I wonder wha

Instincts told Conrad that Audrey wanted to kiss him, too.

Gazing at Audrey, he angled his face and kissed her mouth softly but unwaveringly. She kissed him back and seemed to enjoy the kiss every bit as much as he did.

It was Audrey who pulled back when he went to deepen the caress. "That was nice," she said.

"It was very nice," Conrad said. As he relished her taste on his lips, slightly sweet and slightly tart, he knew he wanted more of her.

"Thanks for a lovely dinner and conversation, Conrad," Audrey said.

He smiled. "It was my pleasure. I hope we can do it again soon."

"I'd like that," she said, looking up at him sweetly. "Well, I'd better go check on my daughter."

"Good night, Audrey." Hiding his disappointment, he reluctantly let her go. He fully understood that the good things in life couldn't be rushed. Besides, Conrad truly respected the love Audrey clearly had for her child.

DEVON VAUGHN ARCHER

has the distinction of being the first male to write solo for the Arabesque line with the groundbreaking 2006 contemporary romance *Love Once Again*. The novel went on to become number one among the Top Ten African-American Stories in eHarlequinNews.com. Devon's first romance novel, *Dark and Dashing*, appeared in the 2005 two-for-one volume *Slow Motion*, which received 4.5 stars from *Romantic Times BOOKreviews* and became a *Black Expressions* selection.

Christmas Heat marks the author's debut romance novel for Kimani Romance and is sure to please fans and attract new ones. In writing this heartwarming novel, Devon was inspired by the spirit of Christmas and the gift of giving, along with the thrill of falling in love. He has always been a true romantic and this is reflected in the pages of *Christmas Heat*.

The author lives in the Pacific Northwest, where he is busy at work on his next Kimani Romance novel, *Destined to Meet* (Kimani Romance, June 2008).

CHRISTMAS
HEAT

DEVON VAUGHN ARCHER

 KIMANI PRESS™

ISBN-13: 978-0-373-86047-0
ISBN-10:   0-373-86047-1

CHRISTMAS HEAT

Dear Reader,

Handsome photographer Conrad Pearson and striking portrait artist Audrey Lamour are the main characters in *Christmas Heat,* a contemporary love story destined to tug at your heart strings.

In this enchanting holiday tale, childhood sweethearts Conrad and Audrey are inadvertently reunited in the town of Festive Cove, Washington. Twenty-five years earlier, both experienced the devastating loss of parents in a Christmas Day house fire that had a lasting effect.

The path toward second chances is less than a smooth ride as pent-up hostilities, bad memories, secrets, deception and trust issues threaten to undermine the steamy romance, scintillating chemistry and all-consuming passion that bring the hero and heroine together.

The inspiration for this novel came from a lifetime of witnessing the dreams, drama and romance at Christmastime.

For those of you who believe in the magical joy of Christmas, second chances to reclaim first love and the power of faith, this sentimental journey is sure to please page after mesmerizing page.

I invite readers to share their thoughts on *Christmas Heat* through the eHarlequin.com community, the Kimani Press Web site as well as online book reviews.

And don't miss my next Kimani Romance title, *Destined to Meet,* on sale next year.

All the best,

Devon Vaughn Archer

Dedication

To the one and only H. Loraine, my beautiful dream girl, who still makes my heart flutter; and Jacquelyn V., my dear, sweet sister and a great source of encouragement.

I also dedicate this book to my growing legion of fans that keep coming back for more and inspiring me to continue to deliver exciting, romantic and sensual love stories time and time again.

Acknowledgments

Christmas Heat was an absolute delight to write and I am confident that readers will be thoroughly engaged by this unique and absorbing holiday tale.

Many thanks to editor Mavis Allen for allowing to spread my wings by writing for Kimani Romance, following a successful Arabesque novel with *Love Once Again.*

I thank Linda Gill, as well, the general manager at Kimani Press, who recognized my abilities as a male romance author and provided the opportunity to showcase my talent successfully.

I would also like to acknowledge Demetria Lucas, who discovered me when Arabesque was still part of BET Books, putting me on a path that would lead to Harlequin.

As the most important person in my life and times and a beautiful lady who knows the insides and outs of true romance, thanks to H. Loraine for your role in bringing this latest romantic masterpiece to life and inspiring me for future ones.

Finally, the Man upstairs is always greatly appreciated for giving me the skills to become a writer, along with the many other blessings He has sent my way.

I look forward to a bright future as a novelist and all it entails.

Prologue

Seven-year-old Audrey Beaumont was fidgety on the day before Christmas, filled with anticipation for what tomorrow would bring. As an only child, she had become accustomed to receiving everything she wanted. Except for maybe the little sister or brother her parents had said they were working on.

Audrey kissed and hugged her mother and father good-night, hoping for something extra special from Santa Claus this year as she had been a good little girl.

"'Night, Daddy. 'Night, Momma," Audrey told them with a bright smile on her face.

Her mother, petite with long, thick dark hair, said

cheerfully, "Good night, honey. Now, you be sure to actually go to sleep, hard as it may be, so jolly old Saint Nick can do his business."

"I will, Momma," she promised, fearing that otherwise Santa might arrive and put ashes in her stocking.

"Nightie-night, sugar," her father said. He was a big strapping man with short, gleaming salt-and-pepper hair.

Without knowing why, Audrey ran to them for one last lingering hug before pedaling off to her room. Looking over her shoulder she saw her parents waving as if about to go on a long journey, then hug each other as though they were posing for a picture.

In bed, Audrey's thoughts were nonstop with Christmas morning just hours away. It was her favorite time of year as she had lots and lots of gifts to tear open and got to eat her favorite foods and desserts. When her eyes began to carry a heavy load, she finally fell into a deep sleep.

Audrey awakened to a rustling sound and instinctively realized that there was something wrong. She smelled smoke inside the house.

Panic struck Audrey like a school bully. She lunged out of bed and raced toward the door. But when she opened it, she was driven back by a wall of bright colored flames.

Fear streaked up and down the little girl's spine. Fear that she would be burned alive and in more pain than she could possibly imagine.

   Fear that her parents were still asleep and no one
would come to their rescue.
   The air suddenly became heavy and Audrey struggled to breathe. She ran to the window and opened
it. The screen kept Audrey from being able to stick
her head out. She pushed hard but it wouldn't budge.
She could feel the torrid heat and actually see flames
searing the side of the house, pushing their way up
toward her second-floor bedroom. She began to cry.
   I don't want to die. I have to do something.
   But what can I do?
   Audrey was terrified. She ran back toward the door
and tried to figure out what to do. Were her mother
and father awake? Did they know what was happening?
   She screamed for them as loudly as her small
throat could bellow.
   *Daddy! Momma! Please come and help. Don't let
the fire burn me.*
   Audrey thought she heard her mother or father say
something, but couldn't be sure above the crackling
sound of flames.
   God please save us all, she prayed with an intensity she had never felt before as the warm tears ran
down her cheeks.
   The fire still blocked her path and pushed Audrey
back. She closed the door, hoping to buy time. She
continued to yell for her parents, even as she tried
desperately to get the screen off the window. Her

lungs burned and breathing became all but impossible as she coughed and lurched.

Her head started to spin and the room became fuzzy. Before she knew it, Audrey felt her legs give out from under her. She again prayed that God would spare them from a horrible death.

Her prayers seemed to be answered when Audrey suddenly found herself in the arms of a powerfully built fireman. He was breathing heavily but his voice was calm when he said, "Don't worry, honey, you just hold on tight. We'll get you out of here. Everything will be fine."

Audrey tried to speak, but her aching throat prevented words from forming. She clung to the fireman like a cub to its mother, drifting in and out of consciousness, unsure if they would make it out of the house alive.

It wasn't until she felt fresh air filling her lungs that Audrey realized she was outside and safe. She coughed in heaves, trying desperately to catch her breath. The fireman was still cradling her to his chest. In this early morning hour she could barely make out the man's face beneath a helmet and covered in soot. He was in his protective gear, which was discolored from smoke and squeaked like a wooden floor as they moved away from the house.

He seemed to smile at her. "You're safe now, sweetheart."

"Momma...Daddy," Audrey shrieked when she

did not see them amongst the people who had congregated around the house, like outside the church after service, and seemed spellbound by the fire that continued to burn out of control.

As if alerted that her parents were still in the burning house, the firefighter handed Audrey off to another one and yelled, "I'm going back in."

The other responded fearfully, "You can't, Pearson. It's too dangerous."

Audrey watched as he stormed back to the house, ignoring those who tried to talk him out of it.

She never got to thank the fireman for saving her life. Or for trying his best to save her parents.

It was the last time Audrey would ever see him again, for the man named Pearson died in the fire, along with her parents.

Chapter 1

Audrey Lamour held on to the steering wheel with both hands as she negotiated her Jeep Grand Cherokee down the slippery road en route to Festive Cove Elementary School. It was the same school she had attended as a child. Now she had passed the reins onto her daughter and hoped that Stacy learned as much as she had—and kept on learning right through college and beyond. But Audrey would take one year at a time and even one day, knowing full well that a person could not look too far ahead in life.

She glanced through the rearview mirror at her child, safely settled into her belt-positioning booster seat, and smiled. God had blessed her with the best daughter a woman could ever have. Surely that had to count for a lot, even against the backdrop of Audrey losing her own parents at a young age and Stacy being deprived of a father's love and devotion.

At seven, Stacy was small-boned and tall for her age. Audrey felt that her daughter was a remarkable, well-adjusted girl, considering that she had never known the man who fathered her. He had ended his relationship with Audrey shortly after learning she was pregnant. In spite of this, Stacy was healthy, had excelled in school, seemed happy and was often the one to lift her mother's spirits when they were down, rather than the other way around.

What would I ever do without the one constant ray of light in my life?

Audrey felt emotional at the thought as she neared the school. She couldn't imagine not being there for her daughter in every way. Her own parents had always been there for her, before tragedy struck and she had to learn to live without them.

And vice versa.

She pulled alongside the curb, then reached back to help Stacy extricate herself from the child safety seat.

"Did you bring your homework?"

Stacy pretended to think about it. "Yeah, right here."

"Good." Audrey noted her lunchbox. "So we're all set, then."

"I think so." Stacy climbed out of the car. "Bye, Mommy."

"Bye-bye, baby. Have fun."

Stacy gave her a crooked smile. "I always try to, but sometimes there's just too much to do."

Audrey laughed. "Tell me about it. Don't worry, you'll appreciate everything they put you through one day."

"Yeah, maybe," she said skeptically. "I have to go now."

"Aren't you forgetting something, young lady?" Audrey stuck out her high cheek.

Stacy leaned in and planted a quick kiss on it, giggling self-consciously.

"That's more like it," she said with a twinkle. "I'll see you this afternoon."

"See ya."

Stacy ran off, blending in with the other students. Audrey watched for a moment longer before pressing slowly on the accelerator. As usual, she had a lot on her mind. Apart from work and household chores, Christmas was just a little more than three weeks away. Meaning there was precious little time left to make sure that Stacy's wish list was fulfilled. Audrey made no bones about it. She was spoiling her daughter rotten, just as her parents had spoiled her when she was a little girl. She knew that as a single parent she was probably overcompensating a bit in providing the love and devotion every child should have.

I just hope she appreciates it. I know I did.

Passing by the Festive Cove Fire Department, Audrey thought about the painting of Grant Pearson that she had bestowed them. It was a small thing to give to honor the memory of the firefighter, and a long time coming at that. But she had a feeling he understood and was smiling down on her, at peace with himself.

Audrey's thoughts turned toward her upcoming visit to Grant's gravesite. There was no doubt in her mind that he was watching over her in his own way, just as he had so many years ago when he saved her life and did his best to save her parents.

Audrey picked up her cell phone and called the art gallery where she was delivering a couple of landscape paintings. Like her seascapes, these were more experimental than the classical portraits she had put her heart and soul into. There would be an exhibit at the gallery later on in the month to gauge the public's interest. She could only hope her audience would be receptive to this side of her talents, giving her the confidence in opening up a whole new front in her art career.

Zack Abu, the Ugandan owner of the gallery that represented Audrey, and a fine artist in his own right, answered the phone. "Good day, Audrey," he said with an accent. "Hope you're calling to tell me you have more exquisite Audrey Lamour pieces to show?"

"As a matter of fact, I do," she said proudly. "I'm on my way to you even as we speak."

"Marvelous. I can hardly wait to see them."

Audrey swallowed uneasily, having never really gotten comfortable with the expectation her paintings brought. There was always a part of her that feared they might not measure up and she would have to look for another means of support, heaven forbid.

Ulysses Conrad Pearson drove his rented Range Rover along the winding path, admiring the view from all sides. It seemed never ending. Snow-covered pines and fir trees blanketed miniature mountains like soldiers on the field ready to do battle. Pale blue ice hung like daggers from limestone cliffs at the side of the road. Conrad could almost hear the rush of water behind tumbling waterfalls frozen into works of sculpture and imagined that if he were to look carefully, he might actually see a deer or two running amongst the plethora of frosted birch and maples in the woods.

In the distance, Conrad could see the outline of the Cascade Mountains, almost eerie in their magnificence. The snowy valley and the near-frozen lake below seemed to complete the picture postcard of his surroundings.

It had been nearly twenty-five years since his father had died in the line of duty. Although two others had died in the house fire that morning, a young girl had miraculously survived, thanks to his father's courage and determination.

It was after the tragedy that Conrad had begun using his middle name, somehow making him feel like a different person than the Ulysses left without a father. With no other family in Festive Cove, Conrad and his mother moved away to live with relatives in Charleston, South Carolina. Everyone agreed that was the best thing for a young widow and her nine-year-old son.

Conrad brushed aside the thought as he drove away from the coastal range and headed down the narrow road that would take him into Festive Cove, Washington. At thirty-four, he realized he'd spent the better part of his life doing what others felt was best for him. He'd been forced to abandon the only real home he'd ever known for all the wrong reasons. He had played on the basketball team in high school because it seemed "the thing to do" for a six-foot-three youth who was still growing. By the time he had graduated, Conrad had gained two inches and torn the anterior cruciate ligament in his right knee, ending any possibility of playing pro ball.

At the University of South Carolina, where he majored in photography, Conrad had met and fallen in love with his now ex-wife, Natalee. They had gotten married within nine months of meeting because she had given him an ultimatum. Either he made her his bride or she would return to her native Ethiopia for graduate studies. Three years later they were divorced and regretting what they both realized was a mistake.

Through it all, Conrad had managed to hold on to his one true passion in life: photography. After college he'd moved around a lot, working as a photojournalist and freelance photographer for years before opening up his own studio in Charleston three years ago. His business had become a major success, and his work behind the lens had made him a top choice for models, newlyweds and others who wanted the best photographs for their money and time. Conrad still had the camera he had gotten for Christmas at age eight, keeping it as an indicator of how far he'd come and how much the past meant to him.

Conrad came upon the Festive Cove Fire Department. He choked up at the memory of his father wearing his uniform, seemingly indestructible. He knew now that this was merely a child's fantasy that fell well short of reality. His father had proven to be all too human at the end of the day.

Something I'm very much aware of in my own life.

Conrad sighed and picked up the magazine that he had brought with him from Charleston. It was an issue of *The Portraiture Artist*. He opened to the page that had a picture of his father—Grant Pearson. With its rich texture, depth and character, the portrait almost seemed to bring him to life.

Local artist Audrey Lamour had recently donated the painting to the Fire Department in memory of the man who had saved her life.

The former Audrey Beaumont was seven at the

time and two grades under Conrad at Festive Cove Elementary School. Audrey was the first girl he had ever kissed. Or had she kissed him first? Neither quite knew what to make of it, but were definitely attracted to each other in the innocent way grade-schoolers found themselves grappling with young romance.

Luckily, Audrey had managed to escape the fire with only a few superficial burns and some tense moments.

The others had not been so lucky.

Conrad gazed at the magazine page again. Audrey had initiated contact with his mother some time ago—exchanging Christmas cards. She had indicated in the last one a desire to do the painting. His mother had provided a photograph to that effect.

Conrad had been less inclined to keep in touch, ignoring Audrey's attempts to reach out. With no one else to vent his frustrations over losing his father, he'd chosen to be bitter toward Audrey, unfair as it were.

Now Conrad only wanted some closure and hoped she could help him to achieve it.

Will coming home again really make any difference this time around?

Guess I won't know till I can sit down and talk to Ms. Lamour face-to-face.

He got back on the road, making a mental note to visit the firehouse once settled in.

* * *

"These are absolutely stunning," Zack Abu declared, eyeing the two paintings Audrey had brought into the gallery.

"You think?" she asked, looking up at her friend in doubt.

Zack was pushing fifty with silvery dreadlocks and a tall, lanky frame. As usual, he was impeccably dressed in a tailored suit and designer shoes.

His gray eyes flickered. "Trust me when I tell you that these landscapes will go quickly, as do all your paintings."

Audrey blushed, pushing aside worries the public would reject her paintings. She was grateful a local gallery was willing to put her works on display with such enthusiasm.

"Well, in that case," she told him, "guess I'd better try to do some more landscapes."

"That's an excellent idea," he agreed. "So long as you keep making collectors enormously happy with the fabulous portraits you do so well."

"Don't worry, Zack, I intend to," Audrey promised. "At least until I've saved up enough money to make sure Stacy and I can live comfortably for the rest of our lives," she added with a wink.

Truthfully, Audrey doubted she would ever give up painting portraits as long as she could lift a brush. Her talent had been given to her for a reason and she intended to use it to the best of her ability.

"How's the little one anyway?" Zack thought to ask.

"Growing up way too fast." The thought of Stacy becoming an adult and living her own life was more than a little nerve-racking to Audrey at the moment.

"Aren't we all?" Zack twisted his lips, looking a bit weary.

Audrey smiled and wondered if she'd grow old alone. A brief marriage to Stacy's father—who had left her to raise Stacy all alone—hardly constituted that once-bitten, twice-shy adage. She preferred to think that if the right man came along, another marriage was possible. Right now, though, she would settle for a nice romantic relationship with someone who could hold her interest and dazzle at the same time, while being trustworthy and respectful.

Audrey watched as Zack hung up the paintings. She had titled one of the new ones "Our Land" and the other "Nature's Beauty." The names seemed to be apropos for what she hoped to present in the works.

After agreeing upon the value of the paintings and a few minutes of chitchat, Audrey was on her way to buy some art supplies and Christmas presents. With any luck, she might actually get to do some painting before it was time to pick up Stacy from school.

Conrad took the cell phone out of his twill jacket and dialed his mother's friend, Lucille Vale. She had generously offered him the use of her home during his stay while she traveled overseas.

"Hello, this is Lucille," the woman said in a high-pitched voice.

"Hi, Lucille. This is Conrad Pearson."

"Oh, hello, Conrad." Her tone perked up. "Are you in town?"

"Just got here."

"Wonderful! The key is under the mat, in case you forgot. Please, make yourself at home."

"I will, thanks."

"Do you need directions on how—?"

"I think I can find it."

"All right. Have fun."

Conrad said he would, but he certainly didn't see this as a vacation. In fact, if everything went as planned, he would be back in Charleston in no time.

As in previous visits, Conrad drove to his childhood home for old times' sake. The bungalow had changed little over the years besides the current copper coloring, which had once been a dull sage. A dusting of fresh snow sat on the porch steps and grass as if to welcome him home.

A touch of nostalgia gripped Conrad like a fever and he recalled the memories of living there with his mother and father.

Unable to handle much more reminiscing, Conrad headed toward Lucille's place.

Chapter 2

Conrad looked up at the large English Tudor-style home, with its brick-and-stone chimney and arched porch entranceway. *If the inside is even half as nice, it should at least make the accommodations pleasant during my stay in Festive Cove.*

Surrounding the house were mountain ash and snow-white flowering dogwood trees. Conrad could imagine how pretty they would look when blossoming in the spring.

Not that he would be here that long.

Conrad found the key and went inside. He was not disappointed in the least. It was clean and spacious with French provincial furnishings, a gourmet

kitchen and a master suite with an incredible Gothic
revival bed.

Now, if only a pretty lady came with the territory...

But that would be getting greedy and maybe just
a bit unrealistic considering he wasn't there for romance. Or even a one-night stand.

Not to say that being alone was Conrad's preference. He wished it had been different at this point in
his life. But what could he do? He'd tried marriage
and that had failed miserably. Maybe that was a sign.
The deck definitely seemed to be stacked against
him when it came to family and all it stood for. And
he'd had nothing but rotten luck when it came to
finding a woman who could truly be the one of his
dreams.

Audrey negotiated the cart past a display of
graphic-art materials at the art-supply shop. She had
just put some oil paints in the basket when her cell
phone jingled. Opening it, she saw a text message
from her best friend, Regina Poole:

On a break from Xmas deco. Do I tone it down or
go all out? Decisions! R U painting? Call me.

Audrey smiled, putting the phone back in her
purse. She jotted down on her mental list to get back
to Regina and offer her suggestions on her Christmas
decorating. Never mind that she'd been so busy she

had yet to finish decorating her own house. Thankfully, there was still plenty of time.

After grabbing several brushes and some cleaning supplies, Audrey went to pay for her items.

Five minutes later she was back on the road and headed to the store, hoping it wasn't super crowded, She had to pick up Stacy soon. Then they'd planned to place the Christmas wreath they'd made on Grant Pearson's grave, the same way they did every December.

Half an hour after moving into his short-term abode, Conrad was ready to visit his father's grave. He thought about Audrey. *What do I say to her after all these years? Should I resent the fact that her life was spared? Or be happy that my father's valiant efforts were not in vain?*

I'll just have to let things play out and see what happens.

Conrad guided his SUV toward the redbrick church he had once attended regularly with his folks. Though not quite as intimidating as it had once been, a streak of compunction whizzed through him. It had been years since he'd last gone to church—*any* church. Partly, this had been the result of a general disenchantment toward religion and faith once his father had died. Partly Conrad blamed his absence from church on a workload that at times had taken over his life almost to the exclusion of everything else.

He drove past the church and on to the cemetery. It was small compared to those in Charleston and had clumps of snow here and there like mounds of earth dug for burial. He could only imagine how many others had joined his father in eternal rest.

Grant Pearson had been buried with honors by the Fire Department and Conrad recalled what a sad day it had been for all in attendance. But mostly for his mother, who had tried to be strong for him, but was never quite the same since the day of the fatal fire.

And frankly, neither was he.

Conrad parked off to the side and began to walk up the hill. The landscape had changed and there were more plots and gravestones to sort through, a map of the macabre. Before long he came upon his father's final resting place.

Conrad noticed there was a woman standing there with a young girl. The woman looked to be in her early thirties. She was tall and slender with dark shoulder-length hair. The girl was no more than seven or eight and she clung to her mother, he assumed, as if afraid she would be left alone.

Conrad recalled that his mother had told him that Audrey Lamour had a daughter and, like him, was divorced. The closer he got to the two, the more Conrad began to recognize that he had stumbled upon the very girl his father had rescued from the fire. The same one Conrad had shared a tender kiss with so long ago, now all grown up with a child of her own. Mixed feelings of bitterness, nostalgia and sorrow left him reeling. There was so damned much he wanted to say and needed to hear; yet he was just as unnerved at the prospect as he was eager to move forward.

In that moment it tugged at Conrad's heart to know that Audrey still cared enough to visit his father after all these years.

When she turned his way, Conrad caught sight of her face which he'd seen in a photograph that clearly didn't do her beauty justice. *Halle Berry meets Beyoncé Knowles in Festive Cove, Washington.* Only Audrey was even more attractive, if that were possible. The years had been very kind to her in that respect.

"Hi," she said in a soft voice.

"Hello," Conrad responded in a tone that didn't sound like his own.

The girl looked up with squinting brown eyes, but did not speak.

"Are you here to visit Grant…?" Audrey inquired with a curious gaze.

Conrad doubted she knew who he was since he told his mother not to send pictures. While he very much wanted to talk to her about his father and how he'd impacted her life, now seemed neither the time nor the place. He didn't want to intrude upon their paying their respects and grieving. Selfishly, he didn't want their presence to interfere with his own chance to mourn. Obviously, Audrey did not recognize him as the short, pudgy boy who once had a crush on her. Probably best to leave it that way for now.

"Uh, no," Conrad answered unevenly. "I'm just headed over there..." He pointed to a nearby grave with a marble headstone twice the size of his father's.

"Oh." Audrey looked embarrassed. Had she perhaps presumed him to be Grant Pearson's son, but now had to rethink this?

Conrad briefly reconsidered if it was a wise thing to deceive her right off the bat, but he was not prepared to confront Audrey in a cemetery of all places. And not with her little girl present. Changing his story now would only make things worse. There would be plenty of time later to try and explain.

At least he hoped so.

Again it struck Conrad how lovely she had become since he had last seen her. Back then she was rail thin and wore her hair in thick pigtails. Though he couldn't see much beneath her long coat, something told him that she was shapely. This fascination was balanced against the deep regret Conrad felt at the paths their lives had taken.

He sighed. "Well, I'd better not keep her waiting any longer."

"You're probably right. Though I suspect that, like Grant here, she's got a lot of time on her hands and will always be there in spirit whenever you can come."

Conrad watched Audrey smile gently, as though she couldn't resist. She was trying to make him feel better. Instead he felt worse for pretending to be there for someone other than his father, while she was apparently comfortable filling in for his absent family.

"Goodbye," Conrad said.

Audrey favored him with a weaker smile and returned her attention to the gravesite she stood before.

As he walked away, Conrad heard the girl say in a friendly voice, "Bye, mister."

He turned and saw a big grin on her face as she waved at him. It was only then that Conrad realized that she was the spitting image of her mother at around the same age. He smiled before quickly moving to the grave with the large headstone.

After a few minutes of waiting his turn to visit his father's grave, Conrad heard Audrey tell her daughter, "We'll come again when we can. Let's go, Stacy."

Resisting the urge to look, Conrad listened to their shoes crunching in the snow like dry leaves. Only when the sounds became distant did he turn to find the two nearly out of the cemetery and back to the land of the living.

He waited a bit longer as if glued to the spot, glancing at the gravestone of the person buried beneath him. It was a woman who had died just five years after his father, at the age of twenty-three. Conrad wondered how she had died and if anyone ever came to visit her. On this day someone had. He hoped she was at peace in the afterlife.

Conrad walked to his father's burial site and saw the wreath of holly left behind by Audrey. The small granite headstone showed signs of wear and tear, but the engravings on it were still as deep and clear as the day his father had been laid to rest:

Grant Jordan Pearson
A Loving Husband and Father
Who Gave His Life to God
In the Line of Duty

"It's been a little while since I was last here, Daddy," Conrad lamented, flashing back to his youth and finding this more difficult than he imagined it would be. "Hard to believe that I'm now the same age you were when you died. Time really flies."

His eyes watered. "It's been hard growing up without a father. There have been plenty of times when I could have used your wisdom and advice."

Conrad wiped at his eyes with a gloved hand.

He apologized for blaming his father for doing his job. If he hadn't, that little girl with Audrey might never have been born, for Audrey would never not have lived past seven years of age herself. Something good had come out of his father's death, even if Conrad wanted so much for things to have turned out differently.

"I miss you, Dad," he cried. "Momma misses you, too."

Conrad touched the headstone, feeling the numbing cold even through his glove. At the same time, he somehow felt his father's spirit, which warmed Conrad's soul.

He walked away believing the first steps had been taken toward the closure he desperately needed. Now he wanted to spend some time with Audrey Beaumont Lamour—the only other person alive, aside from Conrad's mother, whose life intersected with his at a critical juncture in time, altering their futures forever.

Chapter 3

On the way home from the cemetery, Audrey mused about how tingly it always made her feel to visit Grant Pearson's gravesite. It was almost as if he were passing on a message from her parents, saying, *Everything will be all right for you and Stacy.*

This was something Audrey very much wanted to believe. *My daughter is pretty much the whole world to me. We've already survived a lot and hope to successfully take on all the other challenges that lie ahead.*

She peeked in the rearview mirror and saw that Stacy had drifted off to sleep, perhaps the culmination of a busy day at school and the emotional drain of visiting deceased grandparents and a firefighter she never knew.

Audrey thought of her landscape paintings on display at the gallery. She was happy that Zack had expressed such confidence in her. She imagined that someday the land- and seascapes would be in as much demand as her portraits, noting that it wasn't so long ago that those, too, had struggled to find an audience.

The words *struggling artist* once seemed as if they were created specifically to describe Audrey. While attending the School of Visual Arts in New York City and WICE in Paris, she had worked the typical low-end jobs to make ends meet. She never knew she could survive on such a tight budget.

With time, patience and perseverance, Audrey graduated from school and her talents began to manifest themselves on canvas and in commercial art. She specialized in classical portraiture, but also used impressionist techniques for capturing the proper design and composition in her artwork.

Her big break as an artist came four years ago, when Audrey beat out many others in being chosen by the Washington State governor to do his family portrait. It was an honor for Audrey to have such an opportunity. She couldn't pay for that type of publicity. As a result of it, she now had subjects coming to her rather than the other way around.

If only her parents had been alive to see her success as an artist. And to see their granddaughter. Audrey winced as though hit in the stomach. Would she ever stop feeling that painful jab when she thought of her parents and Grant Pearson?

Audrey was thankful to have been adopted by a kind and devoted couple who became her parents after years of being unable to have children of their own.

Audrey counted her blessings time and time again. Unfortunately, these blessings did not include men, whom she'd had little success with thus far in life. She'd met Stacy's father while living in New York. Thinking she was in love and finding Julius Lamour the most handsome man she'd ever laid eyes on, Audrey had jumped into bed, then marriage, without ever truly knowing the man who became her husband. Not until it was too late. Julius never felt that the word *faithful* applied to him, romancing other women whenever it suited his fancy. Things came to a head as soon as he realized she was pregnant. He quickly decided that his wife and child had no place in his self-centered life. Divorce followed shortly thereafter, along with the pain of single motherhood and the struggles of trying to raise a daughter alone.

Other men had not been much better, making Audrey sometimes believe that she was destined to have to do without quality male companionship for the rest of her life. But she did have Stacy and her art to keep her from feeling lonely. And she still had hope.

For whatever reason, Audrey's ponderings turned to the man she had seen at the cemetery. Only a few words had passed between them, but she thought there was something oddly familiar about him. He was tall, good-looking, with a sexy shaved head and well-developed body. Could they have met before? Or was that simply her imagination at work?

Yes, that must be it.

Loneliness had a way of doing that to you. Since the man gave no indication of knowing her—even if his ebony gaze had bored down on Audrey like a ray of heat—obviously they were nothing more than strangers and unlikely to cross paths again. Probably for the best.

Conrad entered the firehouse, and got a funny feeling, as he had during previous visits. He gazed at the framed photographs of firefighters, past and present, adorning the lobby walls like decorations. It took only a moment to spot his father's picture. Conrad thought of how young his father looked compared to his own boy's memory of him seeming so much older.

Then, on the other wall, Conrad noted that the centerpiece was the painting Audrey had done of his father. He took a closer look at it, admiring the colorful and surreal portrait. His heart skipped a beat in that moment as Conrad reflected on his father's ultimate sacrifice.

"Can I help you?" a deep voice asked.

Conrad turned and saw a husky man around his age and height with blond micro-braids and a goatee. He wore casual firefighters' work attire and was holding a mug of coffee.

"Actually, I just came in…well, I guess for old times' sake," he responded unevenly.

The man lifted a thick brow. "You used to work here?"

"Not exactly. My father was a fireman here. He used to bring me in to see what he called his home away from home."

"Just how long ago are we talking about?"

"Twenty-five years," Conrad said matter-of-factly.

"Wow. That does go back more than a few years. What's your father's name?"

Conrad gazed at the painting bearing his image. "Grant Pearson."

"Pearson." The man flashed him a look of familiarity and sorrow. "My own father worked here back then and knew yours. He was a good man from what I've been told. So you must be…?"

"Con—um, Ulysses Pearson."

"I'm Willis McCray." He stuck out a hand and Conrad shook it. "I think we may've known each other back in the day as two little troublemakers."

Conrad remembered the name. "Yeah, I could see that. Most firefighters' families seemed to pretty much stick together at town functions, picnics and whatnot."

"That hasn't changed any through the years," Willis said proudly. "So where you been, man? If I remember correctly, you and your mother moved to South Carolina."

"To Charleston, actually."

Willis's lower lip hung open. "And you haven't been back here since?"

"A few times." Conrad wished it had been more, all things considered—including Audrey.

Conrad watched as another man in uniform, maybe ten years his senior, entered the lobby.

"Thought I heard someone mention the name Pearson," the man said.

"This is Grant Pearson's son," Willis said. "Ulysses, our fire chief, Hamilton Long."

Conrad shook his hand. "You knew my father?"

"Only by legend, which has grown since Audrey Lamour's painting was hung."

Conrad marveled at the notion, certain his father would have approved. "He loved his job." Something that Conrad could not always appreciate when young. Even now he questioned why his old man didn't choose a less hazardous occupation.

"You have to love it to be a firefighter," Hamilton said. "But then the same is true for anything you put your heart and soul into."

"I suppose so."

After Hamilton left, Willis asked, "So what brings you back here this time around?"

Conrad raised his eyes to the portrait. "I heard about that and wanted to come see it myself."

Willis looked at the painting. "The artist did a hell of a good job."

"I agree."

Conrad considered his brief exchange with Audrey at the cemetery earlier. He wondered if she had somehow been able to see right through him and recognize that he had been a childhood schoolmate and was the son of Grant Pearson. If so, she had not indicated such, making him feel all the more foolish for not putting his cards on the table from the start.

"So what's her story?" Conrad asked as a means to pick up some tidbits on Audrey that could help his cause.

"Audrey was the little girl your father rescued from that burning house," Willis said, his brows knitted. "Of course, you may already know that."

Conrad remained silent.

"Yeah, anyway, that's her. After what had to be a difficult stretch for a while there, losing her own parents and all, she went on to become a big-time artist."

Indeed, Conrad already knew that much. Aside from what Audrey had shared with his mother about herself, he had done some Internet research on her. She was a successful and internationally recognized portraiture artist. Apparently most of Audrey's paintings required sittings by the subjects and there was a long waiting list. But she had somehow found the time to paint his father.

"Well, I'm glad she honored my dad this way," he said, glancing again at the painting.

"It's a tribute to the whole department," Willis voiced. "Everyone who comes in here always notices the painting and appreciates the sacrifice your father and others have made as firefighters doing their job as part of this community. They understand we really do put our lives on the line to help others."

Conrad was happy to hear this. He never wanted his father to be forgotten by those he served and worked with. Maybe the painting was a godsend.

He locked eyes with the firefighter. "Guess I'll have to thank Audrey personally for immortalizing my father in a way no one else could have."

"Good luck. Don't really know the lady that well, outside of her generous donations to the Firefighters' Fund and giving us the painting of your dad, but I'm sure she'd be glad to meet you. I suspect you two probably have a lot to talk about."

"I suppose so." But where to start was the big question for Conrad. He would simply play it by ear. He had no intention of leaving Festive Cove till he spoke to Audrey Lamour about that fateful morning.

That night Conrad phoned his mother. She had not been in favor of his returning to Festive Cove and, as she put it, "reopening old wounds." Before Audrey had reached out to her, his mother had dealt with her own grief by pushing it away as if it were a stack of old newspapers she would just as soon not read again.

Maybe he had done the same thing, which was why Conrad wanted to face what had burdened him—and what he had for so long tried to run from.

"I visited Dad's grave today," Conrad told her while seated on a wicker chair in the sunroom of his rented house, beer in hand.

"Oh, Ulysses, why do you insist on putting yourself through this?"

"Through what, Momma?" he dreaded to ask.

"Searching for answers where there are none! Your father, bless his soul, is dead and comfortably in heaven now. Going to his gravesite again to talk to dirt and granite will not change that any."

Conrad frowned. "Maybe not, but at least it'll make me feel closer to him in a way I've never been able to in Charleston."

His mother gave a heavy sigh. "You're as stubborn as your father was, boy. He never listened to me, either, unless he felt it was to his benefit."

"I wish he'd never gone out that Christmas morning," Conrad said sadly. "Then things might be different."

"We don't know that," she said. "Your father did what he had to do, what he'd done for years and was one of the best at. It nearly killed me to lose him, but son, I knew his line of work when I married him. I would have never wanted to change him, despite the fact my heart stopped every time he was called to a blaze. And that Christmas morning, well, it was just his time to go."

"Yeah, I suppose." Conrad hated to believe that was true, but couldn't argue with the facts as they were. Including that Audrey Beaumont had escaped the same fate and was still alive to talk about it.

But will she talk about that painful time in her life with me?

Or would she reject his need for answers and solace.

"I just don't want you to get hurt, Ulysses," his mother told him with feeling. "I loved your father dearly and always will. God knows that. But it's way past time to let him go and live your own life. He would want that."

"I know, Momma." Conrad choked back tears. "I just want to make my peace with Dad and his death in my own way. Can you understand that?"

He could only hope so, for the last thing Conrad wanted was to alienate the only parent he had left. They needed each other.

She gave a long pause and then said, "Yes, I can and I'll always support you, son. You know that. All I ask is that you don't expect anything unrealistic to come out of your journey of self-discovery."

Conrad pondered if it was truly unrealistic to think

that he might be able to somehow come away from this with a greater sense of identity, belonging and purpose. Or was he only setting himself up for failure and a great sense of dissatisfaction?

"Did you talk to Audrey yet?" his mother asked, her voice brimming with curiosity.

Conrad paused thoughtfully. "No, I haven't had a chance to."

Certainly not in the way that he wanted. But at least he had broken the ice a bit by exchanging a few words with the lady.

"Well, be gentle with her, son," his mother said. "Remember that she lost *two* parents that morning. It can't have been any easier for her than you all these years."

"Yeah, I'm aware of that." Conrad wished he could keep the focus on his own loss, not hers. But that wasn't really possible, was it? Whatever unfair resentment he may have once felt for Audrey, she'd surely had a rough go of it, as well, all these years. "I have no intention of trying to ruin her life by blaming her for Dad's death."

Easier said than done. Who the hell else could he put the onus on?

Conrad rejected this reasoning, hard as it was. Though he'd long wanted to place the blame on someone, from what he understood, the cause of the fire had been faulty wiring. Meaning that Audrey Beaumont had been just as much a victim as her parents and his father.

He would do well to keep reminding himself of this as the time drew near for him to meet Audrey face-to-face for a conversation that was long, long overdue.

Chapter 4

After taking Stacy to school the next day, Audrey
came right back home to the two-story Victorian that
served as her residence and studio. It had been given
to her by her adoptive parents who were retired and
living in Palm Springs. She hoped to one day pass it
along to her own daughter. Built nearly a century ago
of Douglas fir with redwood siding, it had a steeply
pitched, hipped roof with cross-gables. A pair of
square columns supported the wraparound portico and
there were two matching brick chimneys. White
spruce and red pine trees stood tall on both sides of the
house.

Audrey picked up the newspaper and headed

down the stone path flanked by uneven layers of snow. The front door was bordered by identical bay windows with matching arched windows above. She entered the house, which had been remodeled more than once over the years, including her own renovations since returning to live in Festive Cove.

Walking across the main floor of hickory hardwood, Audrey found herself admiring the place, much as she did when she first came to live with Oliver and Loretta Sinclair, shortly after her parents' death. She remembered being in awe of its sheer size and its interesting curves and angles. Now in the living room, she glanced up at the high ceiling and custom crown molding before turning to the woodburning fireplace with tile mantel and hearth. The eclectic arrangement of contemporary and country furniture was enhanced by a grandfather clock and accent rugs.

Audrey walked over to an area in front of stained-glass windows and turned on the Christmas tree lights. She had long found this time of year particularly difficult, but she fought back her regrets so that her daughter did not associate the celebration of Christmas with death and despair.

She passed through the French doors leading to the formal dining room with its brass chandelier and period wallpaper. The antique furniture included a mahogany corner cabinet and oval dining table.

Audrey had completely updated the kitchen with

all new appliances, custom-built glass front cabinets, granite countertops and a butcher-block island. The adjoining breakfast room was connected to the terrace and had a cherry trestle table with faux-leather stools.

She headed back through the house, which had been further modernized with smoke detectors and a security system. Her eyes took in the oak hand-carved staircase in the foyer with its wide, curved steps. An ornate brass balustrade lamp was built into the banister. She made her way down a long hallway before coming to what was formerly the family parlor and had been transformed into her art studio.

Though maintaining many of its original architectural details and its openness, the room was now about creation and artistic expression. Paintings were in various stages of completion and the magic tools of the trade were ever present.

Audrey's reverie was snapped when she heard the doorbell ring. She had no appointments scheduled for today, but didn't rule out someone getting their appointments mixed up. Either that or Regina had gotten bored and decided to drop by unannounced.

After brushing some errant curly strands of hair into place, Audrey opened the door. It took her only an instant to recognize the handsome man standing there as the one she had seen yesterday at the cemetery.

Audrey took a moment to study him in greater detail as if a subject to paint. He was very tall, fit and bald with sharply defined, gentle features. Beneath dark brows, gray-brown eyes stared back at her with recognition. She had gotten a similar feeling at the cemetery the day before, but figured she had just been imagining things.

And maybe she was. After all, wouldn't she remember if they had met before?

"Hi." He spoke in a strong and steady voice with a southern accent. "Hope I didn't catch you at a bad time."

She raised a brow suspiciously, ignoring the fact that he was an artist's dream. This still didn't prevent her from being wary. "That depends... Do I know you?"

Conrad wasn't sure how he should respond. He'd waited so long for this moment—and avoided it so long—that it only made sense to tell her the truth. Certainly she'd understand that, unsure of how things would unfold, he hadn't wanted their first meeting in twenty-five years to happen in front of her little girl. Yet he just wasn't ready for the conversation he knew needed to take place. It wasn't right for him to continue letting Audrey think that they weren't connected, but whether it was the fear of the emotions he'd locked away for so long, or the sudden desire to learn about her and how she'd survived, he just wasn't ready to talk about the death of their parents or disclose his own painful struggles.

"We met at the cemetery, sort of," he said. *And*

before that many blue moons ago. He noted that without the oversized coat on, she did indeed have a nice figure to go with her beauty.

Audrey flashed bold eyes at him. She hoped he wasn't a stalker or someone who hung around grave-yards for reasons that had nothing to do with re-specting the dead.

"I remember." She waited to see just where this was going.

"After you walked away I realized who you were." He took a clipping out of his pocket and showed it to her.

Audrey's heart skipped a beat when she saw a small photograph of her face next to the painting of Grant Pearson that she had presented to the Festive Cove Fire Department.

"I subscribe to *The Portraiture Artist,*" he said equably. "I've always admired artists with the talent to paint portraits. The write-up had your studio info in it."

"Oh, I see." Audrey realized the man was clearly interested in her artwork, not in hitting on her. The fact that he also had an intriguingly nice look about him to her trained artist's eye—not to mention her re-sponse to him as a woman—didn't hurt matters any.

"My name's Conrad."

"Audrey Lamour," she said routinely, though evi-dently he knew exactly who she was.

If she noticed that he'd left off his last name, she

didn't comment on it. Conrad stretched a long arm
and extended a large hand. *Hard to feel bitter toward
someone who looks as great as she does.*

Audrey shook his hand and was amazed at how
warm it felt, like being enclosed in a slightly cal-
loused mitten.

"Nice to meet you, Conrad." Her mouth widened
into a dazzling smile.

"Same here."

Conrad put the clipping away. "I'm sure you do
things by appointment and I probably should have
called first, but since I was in the area—"

"It's fine." Truthfully, Audrey sometimes wondered about the wisdom of having an in-home studio
and advertising it for anyone to show up uninvited.
But as an artist raising a seven-year-old alone, it was
a practical way to go at this time in her life. She could
work and be near her daughter on Stacy's time away
from school. She looked up at him. "So how can I
help you?"

Conrad met her eyes steadily. Instead of saying what
was really on his mind, he responded, "I'd like to talk
to you about commissioning a portrait of myself."

Must mean he has a lady, thought Audrey, feeling strangely disappointed. Why else would he want
a portrait of himself, even if he was really easy on
the eyes? Surveying his chiseled, totally masculine
features, she salivated at the idea of putting him on
canvas. Problem was, her client list was already full

for the foreseeable future as lately Audrey had been in hot demand.

"I don't come cheap," she warned him. "Depending upon the subject, location, timing and other factors, my portraits usually go for several thousand dollars." She may as well be upfront with him so as not to waste either of their time.

A half grin appeared on his face. "I gathered that I'd have to shell out some bucks. Price is not a problem for me. I'm far more interested in finding a portrait artist who knows what she's doing. If your painting of the firefighter in the magazine is any indication of your talent, then I'm sure I've come to the right artist."

Audrey felt flattered. She hadn't exactly done the piece in *The Portraiture Artist* for the promotion, but rather as a sincere tribute to Grant Pearson and his heroic attempt to save her family. If it led to new clients, then all the better.

"Have you seen any of my actual portraits, Conrad?" she asked.

"Can't say that I have," he admitted.

"You can find some on display at the Beauty In Art gallery."

Conrad recalled passing it on the way into town yesterday. "I'll have to check it out. Are there any portraits in your studio I can take a look at?"

"Sure." Audrey invited him in, deciding he seemed on the up and up. Prospective clients, even those more familiar with her paintings, usually wanted to see samples of her work before commissioning a painting.

Conrad followed Audrey down the hall. Glancing over his shoulder, he could see that the place was well put together with elaborate architecture and expensive furnishings. He had no idea if there was a man in her life, but was curious. More importantly, he wanted to get a sense of her artistic style where it concerned portraits, over and beyond her painting of his father.

"Here are some of my recent paintings," Audrey said. There were several framed portraits lining the studio walls that she had done of her real and adoptive parents, friends and Stacy.

It was the one of her daughter that especially caught Conrad's eye. Aside from the fine detail and gothic style, it was the fact that the portrait reminded him of Audrey as a little girl. He wondered if she was even aware of the almost uncanny similarities.

"She's very pretty," he commented.

"My daughter, Stacy," Audrey said proudly. "It wasn't easy getting her to stay still for any period of time, but everything worked out in the end."

"I agree."

Conrad thought it best not to linger too much on the portrait, turning his attention to others. All in all he could see that Audrey was definitely an artist with a multitude of talent. He was sure that her parents would have been pleased at what she had made of herself. Just as his father would have been thrilled to know he had made good use of that old camera and the skills he had developed behind its lens.

Audrey observed Conrad as he wandered about the studio like a child amongst his toys at Christmas. She wondered what his story was. Probably married or involved with someone.

Did he have children?

And who was the female he visited at the cemetery? Could be that he'd lost a parent too early in life, too?

All of which is none of my business.

She turned her thoughts back to the moment at hand, which was showing a prospective client a sample of her capabilities. Often it was enough to secure the commission. Would that be the case here, too?

"This is very similar to the painting in the magazine," Conrad said, eyeing a portrait of his father in uniform that was based on a photograph his mother had given her for the firehouse painting. Obviously she had felt compelled to do two portraits.

"A bit," Audrey acknowledged. "The two are similar, but represent slightly different views of the subject."

He nodded. "So who is this person to you, anyway?" he ventured innocently. "I think I caught something in the article about a guardian angel and hero?"

Audrey considered the question. "He saved my

life a very long time ago. Since then, I've had the feeling that he's still watching over me."

"Like a guardian angel?"

"Something like that."

"Interesting."

Conrad regarded the painting again. Was his father truly watching over her? Did he not hold her at all accountable for his death?

Audrey wondered if he thought she was strange. It was not like she was suggesting that Grant's ghost was hanging around or anything, haunting her. His presence was not a palpable but rather a spiritual thing. Much like Audrey felt with her own mom and dad. Maybe Conrad could relate with someone he'd lost.

Conrad gazed at her. "Is he the one you were visiting at the cemetery?"

"Yes, along with my parents."

"I'm sorry about—"

"Don't be. They've been dead a long time, just like Grant."

Conrad winced at the thought. In some ways, it seemed like only yesterday that his father was alive and well.

"Were you there to see a relative?" Audrey decided to ask.

Yeah, a pretty close one. Conrad bit his lip, holding back the truth. "A family friend of sorts."

"I see."

Conrad again looked at the painting of his father and back at the artist. "So these paintings of Grant Pearson are like some sort of catharsis to you?"

"Yes, I suppose you could say that."

In truth, the paintings were much more than that to Audrey. She saw them as a lifeline of sorts in dealing with her feelings in a positive light and a constructive use of her talents in depicting the man who rescued her from the flames of death.

"Well, I think your work is excellent," Conrad told her sincerely. And hauntingly mesmerizing, he thought, as seeing both paintings of his father somehow made him feel closer to him.

"Thank you." Audrey beamed. "I try my best."

"I'm sure you do. I hope I can become a new satisfied client."

"Maybe you can at that."

Audrey saw nothing that made her think he wasn't totally serious. Though she had a backlist of clients, his arresting features were simply too much to pass up putting on canvas.

She walked over to a table and grabbed one of her business cards, came back and handed it to him. "Why don't you give me a call soon and we'll talk about it some more." That way there would be no pressure and ample time to back out should either of them have a problem.

Conrad pocketed the card after reading the information, which included her cell-phone number. "Sounds like a plan."

"Great."

Audrey walked him to the door. He stopped before they reached it and looked into the living room.

"Beautiful tree," he commented, admiring the size along with the ornaments glimmering in the multi-colored flashing lights.

"My daughter picked it out," Audrey said, smiling. "We both decorated it."

"Well, you two make a good team."

She nodded her head in agreement. "Do you have any children?"

Conrad lowered his head. "No. My ex and I weren't ready to go down that road until it was too late."

"Sorry to hear that." Audrey was uncertain if it was anything to be sorry for, knowing that not all people wanted to have children.

"It's all right. Some things just aren't meant to be."

She said goodbye to him at the door and found herself watching him as he walked away and got into his SUV. He seemed nice enough and was divorced. But did that mean he was single and available and looking for something other than an artist to paint his picture?

Audrey thought it best not to get ahead of herself. After all, she wasn't out there pursuing the dating scene these days.

*Why don't I just wait to see if he calls to commis-
sion a painting and go from there?*

Driving away, Conrad almost hated to leave, having enjoyed Audrey's company far more than he
wanted to admit. A twinge of guilt gnawed at him in
not being more forthcoming as to who he was. Particularly when there were so many things he wanted
to ask her about that early morning fire. But it was
clear that Audrey was still dealing with her own
demons and he didn't want to add to them.

*Or have I suddenly lost my backbone in trying to
come to terms with Dad's death once and for all?*

Conrad decided he should try to find out what he
could about his father's last day alive without
stepping on anyone's toes. Or, more specifically, the
delicate toes of Audrey Lamour.

There was no denying that there was something
between them. He sensed that she felt it, too.

For now that needed to take a backseat to the real
reasons he had come back to Festive Cove. It was
how far to probe into it that was his greatest challenge. To go too far could be disastrous for them
both—he really didn't want to come on too strong
with Audrey when it was so clear she was still dealing with the fire. But not going far enough would
leave him with questions he needed answered for his
own peace of mind.

Chapter 5

"How's everything there?" Conrad asked his personal assistant, Jayne Miller, over the phone while he drove. He had essentially taken a leave of absence from his photography studio for this personal journey into his past. Foolish or not, he was going with his gut on this one while hoping his clients did not abandon him in droves.

Who knows, though, he thought. Sometimes being a little inaccessible actually increases demand.

"We're swamped like you wouldn't believe," Jayne complained. A moment later, she said, "I'm just messing with you, Conrad. Of course we're in a bit of a tight squeeze with those clients who insist on being photographed by you instead of one of our other photographers. But everything will be fine. I pushed all of your appointments back and assured everyone who's asked that you are not at death's door or ready to retire, but simply left town briefly for personal reasons."

"Good to see you're right on top of things, Jayne. What would I do without you?"

"Don't ask."

He grinned. "All right, I won't." As it was, Conrad looked forward to getting back home to the great life he'd made for himself in Charleston. But not until he'd achieved the objectives that now seemed to be changing before his very eyes.

"So what exactly are you up to in Festive Cove?" Jayne asked nosily.

Conrad sighed as he rounded a corner. "I told you, I needed to clear up some loose ends regarding my father's death."

"Yeah, I know what you said, but you were never really specific, other than to say that it involved some unfinished business."

"It's a long story that I don't care to get into right now, Jayne," Conrad said. "All you need to know is that I'm fine and will be checking back with you often."

"Got it," she said. "I'll just mind my own business and keep things running as smoothly as I can during your absence."

"I'm counting on that, Jayne. Thanks." He disconnected, then called two of his photographers to make sure everything was up to snuff.

Conrad came to a halt at a red light. He hadn't realized just how much he would miss the photography that had become his whole life in such a short amount of time. He imagined it would be the same if Audrey were to suddenly decide to take a break from painting, only to experience severe withdrawal.

He crossed the intersection and pulled into the lot for Beauty In Art. Seemed like a good idea to see what else Audrey had painted with the second chance at life she'd been given courtesy of his father.

Audrey got a call from Regina after Conrad left.

"What are you up to?" Regina asked.

"Guess?" Audrey sipped on a cup of hot chocolate. "I have seemingly a thousand paintings commissioned—then there's the show coming up. And the art class I teach at the community college has two more weeks before Christmas break. Oh, and did I forget to tell you that I'm slowly but surely grooming Stacy into becoming Festive Cove's next great artist."

"Enough already! I get the point. In other words, you need a *man* in your life."

Audrey cocked a brow. "Excuse me?"

"And a hearing aid, apparently. Come on, Audrey, we both know that there's more to life than work, more work and being a mommy. Especially at Christmas when it's nice to have someone to snuggle up to in front of the fireplace, not to mention under the covers."

Audrey chuckled uneasily. Regina was three years older and on her second marriage. Audrey was still trying to get over her first one. Though that didn't mean she would be close-minded to romance, should it come her way.

"I would love to snuggle with a special man," she admitted. "But *only* if it felt right."

"You won't know till you sample the product."

"Are we talking about men or food?" Audrey couldn't help but laugh.

"I'm on my way to the gym. Why don't you join me? There are always plenty of rock-hard bodies around to catch your eye."

"Are you bringing your husband along for the ride?"

Regina exhaled. "And pull him away from the job? I don't think so. But, hey, there's no harm in looking, right?"

"If you say so." Audrey suppressed a giggle. "Anyway, I'm going to have to take a rain check on that one. I promise we'll go to the gym together soon."

"You know I'll hold you to that."

"I know."

Audrey hung up and tasted her cocoa. She thought about Conrad and wondered if he went to the gym.

Or did he have his own workout routine that he did at home to stay in such good shape?

Conrad walked into the limestone-and-brick building that housed the gallery. He was curious to see more of Audrey's paintings. Maybe they would reveal more about the woman.

The gallery had a warm ambiance to it. Framed artwork of various styles and shapes adorned the walls while pedestals holding sculptures and metal art seemed perfectly situated to the environment.

Conrad passed by a collection of African and Native-American art, followed by folk art and contemporary glass art. Then he came to a set of oil landscapes. One was a dramatic depiction of a city street, complete with buildings, traffic and people seemingly confused over which direction to go. The other was of the countryside with rolling hills of apple-green, tall trees that added to the richness of the setting and a small cottage with a thirtyso-mething man and woman sitting on the terrace, apparently content with the land and in love with each other.

Both landscapes had an ethereal quality that made them all the more appealing. The interesting choice of colors and touch of mystery the paintings embodied seemed to reflect the artist's mood. While not quite sure why, the paintings reminded Conrad of the one Audrey Lamour had painted of his father.

Perhaps because of the uniqueness of the works and the eye-catching fine detail. Glancing at the nameplate beneath the display, he was not entirely surprised to see that Audrey was indeed the artist, and obviously much more of a versatile artist than he had thought.

"Can I help you, sir?" someone asked in a foreign accent.

Conrad looked to his left and saw a man approaching.

"I think I may have found what I was looking for," he responded, glancing back admirably at Audrey's work.

"Ah…yes, Ms. Lamour's pieces. They are quite remarkable. So is she."

Conrad nodded, as if he could vouch for the latter comment in particular. The seven-year-old girl he remembered was cute and bubbly, if not exactly remarkable in his nine-year-old mind. But the current version of Audrey was indeed remarkably appealing from every angle. He had yet to read much into her character and soul beyond the gift of artistry, though he fully intended to.

"My name's Zack Abu. I'm the owner of the gallery and a good friend of Ms. Lamour."

"Nice to meet you. My name's Conrad."

Since Zack Abu was quite a few years older than her, Conrad assumed that when he said *good friend,* he meant it literally. And nothing more. *Where did that come from?* Conrad certainly didn't know

Audrey well enough to judge her choice of companionship. Much less be jealous of another man.

Besides that, Audrey Lamour's personal life was none of his concern. *Just because I'm alone and maybe a little uptight about it doesn't mean I'd wish this on anyone else.* Not even someone who had inadvertently helped to change his life forever.

Conrad felt self-conscious all of a sudden, as if he were on display instead of the paintings.

"So do you think you might like to take one of these dazzling paintings with you today?" Zack asked hopefully.

Looking over them again and eyeing the hefty price tag, Conrad's first thought was a flat no thank you. But in studying the pieces and realizing that he really was smitten by their originality, depth and character, he made an about-face. It might be a good investment to own an Audrey Lamour painting or two. Who knows what they might be worth in ten or twenty years? Perhaps his mother would also find one a perfect fit for her house. Furthermore, it could give him another avenue for communicating with Audrey on a level that wouldn't be too threatening for either of them.

Turning to meet Zack's gaze, Conrad responded, "I think I'll take both of these beautiful paintings off your hands."

He could see that the owner of the gallery could barely contain his enthusiasm. Admittedly, it seemed to be catching as Conrad considered the impact of connecting himself to the artist in more ways than one.

"Got some wonderful news for you," Audrey heard Zack Abu say on her cell phone as she took a break from working on her latest canvas: a seascape complete with a sandy beach, mountains and plenty of sunshine.

"Oh…?" She raised a brow fancifully, knowing that the news could still fall short of ideal. Surely he had not sold one of those landscapes already? Perhaps he had referred someone to her studio for a portrait.

"I just sold *both* of your landscapes!" Zack exclaimed in an I-told-you-so voice.

"That's fantastic…and so quick!" Audrey put the phone to her other ear. She felt truly blessed that her paintings—including the new landscapes—were good enough to command the interest of people; she knew how many artists struggled to find their way in the art world.

"What can I tell you? The man was blown away by the paintings. Not surprised. You are really making a name for yourself, Audrey."

"I guess I am," she said, feeling just a little overwhelmed.

"I think your show in two weeks will be standing room only, mark my word."

"We'll see about that." Audrey never took anything for granted, knowing there was no sure thing in life—except death. She focused on the man who purchased the paintings. Obviously must be a collector. "So who was the buyer? Maybe I can send him a little thank you note."

"Name's Conrad. Haven't seen him around here before but he obviously knows talent when it's staring him in the face."

Conrad. Audrey chewed on that thought. *First a request to do a portrait and then he purchases my landscapes?* Had she really made that much of an impression on him based on her article in *The Portraiture Artist?*

Or was there more to Conrad than met the eye...?

Chapter 6

Conrad brought the paintings back to his borrowed house. He would decide where to hang them later. Right now he was content to simply admire them and think about the woman behind the creativity. Audrey Lamour had obviously pulled herself up from the devastation of losing both parents. Or was she simply better able to mask her scars than him?

Conrad was given a start when his cell phone rang. The caller ID showed it was his best friend, Brandon Spade, phoning from Atlanta, where he worked for the FBI. Brandon had been the best man at his wedding and the one Conrad leaned on for support after his divorce.

"Hello, Bran," he said, shortening Brandon's name as he had since they were in college.

"Hey! What's up, man?"

"Not much. Just trying to readapt to this place. Comes with a lot of baggage."

"Yeah, I hear you." Brandon paused. "You sure going back there again was a good idea?"

Conrad considered the question. Aside from his mother, Brandon was the one person he trusted enough to confide in about the nature of his trip.

"Guess I won't know that till I complete my mission."

"You sound more like an FBI agent than photographer."

"I don't mean to be cryptic," Conrad said. "It's just that I really can't say yet if it was a good move on my part. But I can tell you that the intention was good, no matter how it ends up."

"Well, have you spoken to Audrey yet?"

"We talked."

"And...?"

"And the jury's still out."

"I see. So how does she look in person after all these years?"

"Beautiful." Conrad could not take that away from her.

"Really?" Brandon hummed.

"Absolutely."

"And she doesn't recognize you at all?"

"I've changed a lot since childhood," Conrad said simply.

"Have you told her who you are? Or is that going to be your little secret?"

"Of course I plan to tell Audrey the truth. Right now I'm just not ready." In the meantime, he wanted to continue to feel her out and see where and what it got him.

"Hope you know what you're doing," Brandon warned.

"So do I." Conrad was not one to play games. At first he only wanted to do right by his father's memory and short life span. But that was before meeting Audrey. Now Conrad wasn't sure what he wanted.

That afternoon Audrey picked Stacy up at school, helping her into the booster seat in the backseat of the car before getting behind the wheel herself.

"How was school today, honey?"

"Fine," Stacy spoke with an elongated voice that reminded Audrey of her own as a girl.

"Did you see Abi?" she asked, speaking of her daughter's playmate, Abigail Everly.

"Yeah. We played with other girls in the school-yard."

"That's good to hear." Audrey glanced in the rear-view mirror. Stacy looked warm and cozy in a hooded parka. "I thought that tonight we would go out for dinner."

She decided on the spur of the moment that the meatloaf she planned to make could definitely wait till tomorrow.

Stacy's eyes popped wide. "Where?"

"You pick."

"Okay."

Audrey was sure that McDonald's, Burger King or Pizza Hut would be her top choices. She mentally prepared herself for a bout of fast food with a child who craved the stuff like it was about to go away for good.

After driving around in search of somewhere to eat, Conrad spotted a place called Café Soul Cuisine. Since his stomach was growling, he decided to go for it. He made a left turn and pulled into the parking lot.

The place was busy with other hungry patrons. There was no one to seat you, so Conrad took the first empty table he could find. It was smack dab in the middle of the room. He wasn't too crazy about eating alone in what was basically foreign territory, but since he *was* alone, he didn't exactly have a say in the matter.

Audrey was caught completely off guard by the restaurant Stacy chose. Yes, this was one of her own favorite places to dine, but she'd assumed that her daughter would pick something more kid-friendly.

"Are you sure you want to eat here?" Audrey

asked. They were in the parking lot of Café Soul Cuisine.

Stacy flashed a toothy smile. "I'm sure. They have really good sweet potato pie, but not as good as yours. Besides, next time you can surprise me with your pick."

Audrey laughed. "Aren't you the clever one? It's a deal!"

Once inside, the smell of fresh coffee infiltrated Audrey's nostrils. At a glance there appeared to be no seating available and, for a moment, she thought they might have to find an alternative place to eat.

"There's an empty table," Stacy said, pointing at a table near the center of the restaurant.

Audrey allowed her daughter to pull her in that direction. When they got closer, she realized that Conrad was sitting at that very table all by his lonesome. Was he waiting for his lady? Or did he prefer to eat alone?

She had hoped he wouldn't notice them before they turned around, if only because of the awkwardness of it all. But his eyes locked onto hers, almost as if he had a built-in radar that had announced Audrey's presence in advance.

"Audrey…"

"Hello, Conrad." She tried to make her voice sound perfectly natural. "Looks as though we like hanging out at the same cafés."

"Apparently." He smiled and stood, turning to Stacy. "And who is this pretty young lady?"

"My daughter, Stacy."

"Hey, Stacy."

"This is Mr. Conrad," Audrey told her, hoping she wouldn't get the wrong idea. Though Stacy seemed content with just the two of them, she had indicated on more than one occasion the desire to have a substitute father with her real one out of the picture.

"Hi, Mr. Conrad." Stacy looked up at him with fascination. "You were at the cemetery."

"That's right." He glanced at her mother and back, hoping to downplay this. "And it's okay for you to just call me Conrad," he said, smiling.

"Conrad would like to commission me to paint his portrait," Audrey felt the need to explain how they knew each other.

"Cool." Her daughter gave a big smile.

Conrad nodded. "Yeah, I think so, too."

"I'm sorry, but we thought this table was empty." Audrey looked at the half finished plate of baby backs and mashed potatoes. "Don't let us stop you from finishing your meal—"

"You're more than welcome to join me," he said abruptly. "Unless you were meeting someone else…?"

"It's just us," Stacy said innocently.

"Then please sit," Conrad insisted. "I could use some company."

Audrey wasn't sure this was a good idea. Business and pleasure didn't mix, from her experience. But he seemed sincere and had plenty of room at the table,

in spite of having spread his own meal about hapha-
zardly. She eyed her daughter for the final say,
knowing that Stacy seemed to have amazing instincts
where it concerned men she had dated in the past.
Not that this was a date.

Stacy didn't take long to think about it. "Let's eat
with Conrad, Mommy."

Favoring Conrad, Audrey smiled. "Looks like
you've got yourself some company."

He grinned. "Looks like I do at that."

Audrey sat. *If I didn't know better, I would think
he'd set this whole thing up, as silly as it sounds. Or
is it?* She thought about the landscapes he'd bought
from Zack. Was there anything more to it than being
an art lover? Should she be concerned?

Conrad waited till mother and daughter had taken
a seat before returning to his own. He certainly hadn't
expected this fortuitous opportunity to spend more
time with the woman who had brought him back to
Festive Cove. Might there be forces at work beyond
his comprehension even more determined than he
was to reunite them and their tragic histories?

Sensing that Zack had likely already informed
Audrey of his purchases, Conrad decided he might
as well come clean. "Thanks for telling me about
your paintings at Beauty In Art. The name aptly ap-
plies. I wound up buying two of your lovely scenic
paintings."

"That's a bit much, isn't it?" Audrey met his eyes, though welcoming his interest in her work.

"Yes, but well worth it for anyone who loves and can afford fine art. Zack certainly seemed to concur."

She didn't doubt that for a moment and really had little, if any, reason to be suspicious. "I'm glad you liked the paintings."

"Loved them is more like it. I didn't realize when seeking your services that you were so multitalented with the brush."

Audrey had heard it all before, but somehow enjoyed the compliment. She forked some steamed carrots. "To be honest, I'm fairly new to the landscapes."

Conrad looked at her with surprise. "Never would have guessed."

"I'm slowly but surely incorporating land- and seascapes into my art, wanting to explore new areas."

"You've gotten off to a good start." He eyed her daughter, who was quiet but observant. "And I suppose you're a little artist in the making?"

Stacy giggled. "Yeah, I can paint, too. Not like Mommy, but my friends like what I put on canvas."

"I'm sure they do. Maybe I can see some of your stuff one day?"

Stacy batted her lashes while grabbing a baby back rib. "Can he, Mommy?"

"We'll see." Audrey hoped to temper her daughter's

enthusiasm. Even if Conrad seemed nice enough to go with being very handsome, sexy and an art connoisseur, he was still a stranger. At least he was at the moment. "So what do you do with your time when you're not commissioning and buying paintings, Conrad?"

"You mean, professionally?" he asked over the rim of his wineglass.

"Well, that would be a good place to start." Audrey tried to imagine what line of work he might be in, but drew a blank. She realized it could be anything, including art.

Conrad gazed at Stacy, not wanting her to feel left out of the conversation. Not to mention every time he set eyes on her, it reminded him of her mother at that age.

"What do you think?" he asked her.

She wrinkled her nose. "How about a basketball player?"

"Not a bad guess. Must be the height. I played a little in high school. But those days are long behind me."

Stacy looked disappointed that she was wrong. "Are you a musician? My friend Abigail's dad plays the saxophone."

"Nope, not a musician—though I do love music."

"How about a writer?"

"Wrong again, I'm afraid."

"Do you paint, too?" queried Stacy wide-eyed. Audrey smiled, happy with the way Conrad allowed

Stacy to play with his occupation. She could see that her daughter was thoroughly engaged.

"Close enough," he said. "I'm a photographer."

"Oh, really?" Audrey raised a brow. She would not have guessed him for a photographer.

"Yeah. Been at it for a while now."

"That's cool," gushed Stacy. "I'd like to be a photographer someday…and an artist…and probably a princess, too."

The truth was, Stacy had no idea what she really wanted to do in life at her young age any more than Audrey had at seven. Though the selfish part of her would love to see Stacy become a great artist one day. The idea of Stacy excelling in photography, which was similar in its artistic expression and visual nature, also appealed to Audrey.

Could that explain the strange connection she felt to Conrad? That they were both artistic? Or was there something more?

"So do you work for a newspaper?" Audrey asked curiously before digging into some macaroni and cheese.

"No, I have my own studio." He knew that would elicit a reaction. "I specialize in portrait photography, weddings, babies, magazine shoots, you name it."

"Wow." She pictured him behind the camera.

Conrad helped himself to a bread stick. "Seems like you and I have more in common than either of us realized when we first met." *If you only knew just*

*how much, would it make a difference in the final
analysis?*

"Seems we do." Audrey couldn't help but be impressed. "Where is your studio?" She wondered if he
had set up workspace in his house, much as she had
for her art studio. Or maybe he was set up in the Pearl
District where there were a number of photography
and art studios.

Conrad hesitated, realizing she had been in contact with his mother. He decided to go forward. "It's
in Charleston."

"South Carolina?" Audrey asked, as if Charleston
were anywhere else.

"Yeah," he said, noting her surprise.

Audrey thought of Grant Pearson's widow and
son, Ulysses, who lived in Charleston. It was definitely a small world.

"So you're visiting someone…?"

"Actually, I'm here on business," Conrad
stretched the truth. In fact, it was the personal business of putting his demons to rest at last, so he could
finally be at peace.

"How long will you be in town?" she asked in a
nonchalant tone.

Conrad dabbed his mouth with a napkin, glad
that she hadn't pressed for more on his life in
Charleston. "Long enough to hopefully get this mug
on a canvas." He raised his chin in a silly pose that
caused Stacy to giggle.

Audrey couldn't help but laugh, as well. "We'll have to see about that." She would love to do his portrait, but there were others waiting in line. He would likely be gone before she ever had a chance to get started.

"I'll admit that I'm probably a lot better behind the camera than in front of the artist," Conrad said candidly. "But I'm also a quick learner, and could imagine that painting being the gift of a lifetime."

"That's really nice," Stacy said. "Isn't it, Mommy?"

"Yes, it is." Audrey smiled and felt flattered that Conrad had chosen her as his artist. But her mind was still swirling in another direction. She wondered what type of business he had in Festive Cove. Did it have anything to do with his visit to the cemetery?

And the gift of a lifetime for whom? That special someone in his life?

Maybe I should just mind my own business and leave him to his.

Even if this tall, good-looking gentleman made it very difficult to focus on anything else.

Chapter 7

"He sounds *too* good to be true, once you take away the part about him living in Charleston," said Regina.

Audrey was having her nails done and trying not to get too carried away over a man she hardly knew. This was proving to be a challenge when the man did seem almost perfect.

"Maybe he is," she suggested.

"And maybe he's every bit the person you've described. Even if you had to go visit him in South Carolina, there's worse things that could happen to you, girlfriend." Regina flipped back the long Senegalese twist that got in her face as she stood over Audrey.

It occurred to Audrey that such a visit would give

her the chance to stop in and say hello to Isabelle Pearson, Grant's widow, whom she'd been in touch with. Maybe she could even try to reconnect with Isabelle's son, Ulysses. She quickly did a reality check.

"Uh, I think we're jumping the gun just a bit here." Audrey batted her lashes, wondering if she should have even brought this up. "First of all, Conrad's commissioning me to do a portrait. No one said anything about us dating, much less having a long-distance thing. I've tried that before and it didn't work."

"Can't judge the future by the past, Audrey. If this man is even half of what you've told me—including the fact that Stacy seems totally taken with him—you ought to at least give it a chance to blossom into something really special."

"He's probably got a significant other in Charleston." Audrey found it hard to imagine otherwise. "Who else does one give an expensive painting of himself to for Christmas?"

"Who knows? Maybe his mom. All I'm saying is keep an open mind, Audrey. If Stacy gets good vibes from him, it has to be a positive sign."

Audrey couldn't deny that her daughter had come away from the impromptu dinner get-together two days ago thoroughly impressed with Conrad. It had been up to her to rein in Stacy's youthful fascination and keep her own emotions under control. The truth was that she was attracted to a man who had a whole other life somewhere else, one he would undoubtedly be getting back to sooner rather than later. While her own life was in Festive Cove, with no plans to change that anytime soon.

"There, you're all done." Regina admired her work as a professional manicurist. "So what do you think?"

Audrey glanced up at her friend's narrow face before honing in on her nails, which had been chiseled and painted berry.

"I love them! Another great job, girl."

"They do look good, don't they?" Regina smiled. "Though let's face it, Audrey, for someone as gorgeous as you, your fingernails are probably the last thing a man will notice, good or bad. But it's still better that they look their best. Paint isn't the easiest thing to get off."

"I agree." Audrey smiled, flexing her nails proudly. "As for being gorgeous, well, I'll leave that up to the man in my life to decide and appreciate— if and when he comes along."

"He will—trust me," Regina said. "So, are you coming to choir rehearsal tonight?"

"Wouldn't miss it."

Audrey had been in the choir off and on since she was a little girl, beginning with junior choir. She didn't exactly consider singing to be her strong point, but she enjoyed the harmony, camaraderie and spirituality of performing in church. She found herself wondering if Conrad attended church in Charleston or if he even believed in God.

She pushed back such thoughts, realizing it did no good to speculate. Especially when there was nothing going on between them.

That evening Conrad shaved his head in the bathroom and recalled his dinner with Audrey and her daughter. He had come all this way to talk about the morning of the fire, but for some reason he couldn't. He didn't want to go there with Audrey yet. He couldn't deny how much he enjoyed Audrey's company and he did want to talk to her—just not about the fire.

Conrad ran a wet towel across his head. No matter what he may have felt about Audrey before he came to Festive Cove, he liked her. Maybe more than he wanted to.

I can't allow myself to be engulfed by bitterness and what-ifs anymore.

Conrad checked his appearance once more and was satisfied that it was presentable. He went downstairs just as the doorbell rang. He found himself wishing it were Audrey paying him a visit, but dismissed the notion, realizing she had no idea where he lived.

When Conrad opened the door, he saw Willis McCray standing there.

"What's up, man?" Willis had a grin on his face.

"Hey, Willis." They had exchanged addresses at the fire station. Conrad felt it might be nice to have someone to hang out with while in Festive Cove.

Especially since Willis's father had worked with Conrad's, giving them at least that much in common, aside from being childhood acquaintances.

"Thought you might like to go out for a drink?"

"Sure, sounds good." Conrad stepped aside. "Come on in while I get my wallet."

"Don't waste your time," Willis said with a sweep of the hand. "You're visiting. It's on me."

Conrad couldn't help but smile. He'd almost forgotten what it was like to experience small-town hospitality. What else was he missing?

The choir practiced till their sound was finely tuned and harmonic. Audrey felt as if her throat would surely crack under the demands of the tough and determined choir director. But she refused to fold and instead sought to blend in as much as possible, molding her soft voice to the songs to the best of her ability.

At one point when she upped it a notch to something bordering on mezzo, Regina uttered to the amusement of all, "You go, girl!"

Audrey blushed, while toning it down and staying within her means.

When choir practice was over, Audrey collected Stacy from the clutches of the junior choir director and headed home. Stacy had been blessed with a wonderful voice and had already done a few solos in church. Audrey believed Stacy had inherited this gift from her grandmother. She recalled her mother singing beautiful melodies around the house effortlessly and knew her mother had imagined herself at Carnegie Hall singing before a packed house.

It had been a long day and Audrey was not at all surprised when Stacy fell asleep the moment she hit the sack. She tucked her little girl in and then headed down to the studio. She did some of her best work at night; it was this work that often motivated her during the day.

Audrey felt inspired to take on more of Grant's second painting. It was as if he were reaching out to her. She could only paint Grant when the mood was right—clues seemed to pop into her head as to who he truly was insofar as expressions and the particular nuances that would reflect his character.

Romeo's Bar and Grill was mostly empty as Conrad sat at a corner table with Willis. A pitcher of beer stood between the men and two mugs were half empty. Donny Hathaway's "This Christmas," piped through two overhead speakers.

"So did you ever catch up with Audrey Lamour?" Willis asked after some small talk.

"Yeah, I spoke to her." Conrad compared his current impressions of Audrey to any preconceived notions. She had made a name for herself as one of the top portrait artists around and was expanding her range to landscapes. Yet she was very down-to-earth

and approachable both as a professional and as a
woman. Not to mention she was stunning with more
than a little sex appeal. "Even bought a couple of
Audrey's paintings from the gallery."

"Cool. A bit out of my price range, but I like looking at her work anyway. Especially the painting of
your old man. There's something classical about it."

"I think you're right about that."

Willis favored him. "Bet she freaked out when
you told her you were Grant Pearson's long-lost son
returned home."

*Probably would have, if I'd gathered up the
courage or the desire to tell Audrey the truth from the
beginning.*

Now Conrad was having second thoughts about
divulging his secret. He feared that doing so at this
point would only manifest feelings of guilt and de-
spondency in her, while likely giving him no more
solace in dealing with his father's death. Apart from
that, Conrad found himself enjoying Audrey's company all over again, just like when they were kids.
Only on a level he could only appreciate as a man.
He saw no reason to rock the boat. Particularly when
he could get what he wanted from her without giving
Audrey something she didn't need.

Conrad also saw no reason to disclose any of this
to Willis. "Yeah, she was surprised, but glad to know
that Grant Pearson's chubby little boy had grown up."

"You've both been to hell and back and came out

of it with your heads on straight. Don't know if I could have, had my folks or old man, well, you know…"

Conrad understood all too well. "Not sure how straight my head is these days." He put the mug to his lips. "Do you think I could talk to your father sometime—about my dad? It sure would be nice to hear his thoughts and get some perspective from someone who knew him other than my mother."

"Yeah, not a problem. He'd like that. Dad always talks about the good old days when firefighters took no prisoners in getting the job done day in and day out. He probably has no shortage of stories about your father and how they hung out together on and off the job."

"I'll look forward to it." Conrad hoped he could fill in some of the blanks from his fading memory of his father. He sipped the beer. He imagined having dinner with Audrey Lamour, just the two of them, and getting to know her as a woman. The thought was pleasing.

"A photographer, huh?" Willis looked across the table.

"That's me."

"Been doing that all your life or…?"

"Damn near. Ever since my father bought me my first camera way back when."

"That's cool. Is there good money in it?"

Conrad gave a half smile. He had not become a photographer to get rich, but rather for the pure love of taking pictures and watching people smile when seeing the results of his efforts.

He shrugged. "I'd have to say it keeps me out of the poorhouse without having to look for a real job." The fact that he had invested his money wisely made the profession that much more meaningful.

Willis grabbed a handful of pretzels. "So you and Audrey Lamour are sort of cut from the same cloth, professionally speaking."

"Yeah, I suppose you could say that." Conrad considered that there was even more symmetry between them on a personal level.

"Too bad you're living in Charleston, man. If not, you two could probably hook up with all you could talk about."

"Maybe," Conrad said. Admittedly, the thought appealed to him. The idea of kissing Audrey sounded good right about now. He recalled again the first time their lips had touched. But that didn't mean they would hit it off romantically twenty-five years later. Was that even possible, given the tragedy that threatened to always come between them? "I think we're both pretty wrapped up in our careers these days for anything beyond that."

At least it sounded good. The truth was that he knew nothing of Audrey's romantic life, aside from the fact that she was divorced. It didn't mean she was single and available. No doubt the lady was a good catch.

Just because dating is practically nonexistent in my life right now, doesn't mean it is in hers.

He decided it was best not to go further down this road, and switched the tables on Willis. "What about you? Dating, married, single and not looking, what…?"

"Married with three kids," Willis answered matter-of-factly. "And definitely not looking. Not unless I want my old lady to kill me."

Conrad grinned and raised his mug in toast. He wanted to feel that sense of contentment again, have a relationship with someone who would commit to only him and was not afraid to take a chance. For some reason Audrey Lamour came to mind.

Chapter 8

Conrad awoke with a shudder. Beads of sweat peppered his brow and upper lip. He propped up on one elbow and regained his bearings. He'd just had the same recurrent dream he'd been having since childhood about his father in a fire. Only this one seemed more vivid and frightening than ever—even though he hadn't been at the scene of the fire that took his father's life.

Conrad wondered if this latest nightmare had anything to do with his being back in Festive Cove. Or could it be related to the fact that he had come into contact with the last person whose life his father saved?

Are you trying to tell me something, Dad? Or am I just still being haunted by the past?

He went down to the kitchen for a glass of water. It soothed his dry throat. In the shadows of the living room, Conrad gazed at the landscapes Audrey painted that leaned against the walls. He knew that no matter what, she deserved to live and explore her God-given talent. He only wished that his father and Audrey's parents had lived to see it.

Audrey was cleaning up and thinking about what Stacy wanted from Santa that year when her cell phone rang. She smiled when seeing that the caller was Conrad.

"Hello, Conrad," she said in a level voice.

"Hope I didn't catch you between brush strokes."

"You didn't. I was just cleaning up the studio."

"I see." He paused. "I was hoping we could get together and discuss the painting."

"All right," she was quick to agree. "When?"

"How about over dinner?"

Audrey was mildly surprised. She had to be certain his intent was what she suspected. "Are you asking me out on a date, Conrad?"

"Yeah, I guess I am. Unless, of course, you're already seeing someone—"

"I'm not." She waited an appropriate beat. "Dinner sounds fine."

"I was thinking that we could try a supper club not far from you called The Creekside Retreat."

"I know the place," Audrey said, though she had never been to it. "Sounds good."

"Does six o'clock tonight work for you?" Conrad asked.

"Six it is. I can meet you there—"

"Or I can pick you up. That's my preference."

Audrey had almost forgotten what it was like to have a man actually want to pick you up for a date rather than have to ask him. Obviously Conrad was not the typical man she'd run across. A good step in the right direction.

"Well, if it's your preference…"

"Wonderful. Of course, you're free to bring Stacy along, too."

The invite of her daughter caused Audrey's heart to leap, even if she was sure he was merely being thoughtful. Most men she had dated had been just the opposite when it came to including the most important person in Audrey's life.

Another plus for Conrad.

"Thanks, but Stacy would probably end up bored to death being with us grown folks. Let me see if I can get a sitter."

Actually Audrey was sure her daughter would jump at the chance to go to dinner with them. Or, more specifically, to see Conrad again, whom Stacy was clearly taken with. But Audrey wanted to get to know the man one on one before letting her daughter become too attached.

"That's perfectly understandable," Conrad said. "So I'll see you at six unless I hear otherwise."

"I'll be ready."

Audrey hung up. She wondered about Conrad. Beyond appearing to be the perfect gentleman and someone she felt a kinship with, what was his background? What type of life did he have in Charleston?

Who is the painting for?

Conrad felt like a teenager going on his first date as he got ready. He hadn't actually meant for it to be a real date, per se, but had jumped at the chance, as if passing up a romantic dinner with Audrey Lamour would amount to failure. As it was, the circumstances might make it easier for him to delve into a topic that might otherwise seem out of bounds: his father's last day on earth.

Beyond that, Conrad really did want to get to know Audrey and he wanted her to get to know him. Or at least as much as he felt ready to share at this point. He truly wanted to put the past behind him and move forward with his life, but some wounds still felt a bit too raw—even after twenty-five years.

Conrad grabbed his keys and headed out the door.

Chapter 9

The Creekside Retreat had a Renaissance-era decor with barrel-vaulted ceilings, brick archways, European antique furnishings and tapestry uphol-stered seating. A brightly lit, beautifully decorated Christmas tree flashed colorfully next to a fireplace with a blazing fire. A pianist played soft standards on a baby grand piano in the lounge.

Audrey listened while Conrad ordered for both of them. Roasted breast of chicken and marinated carrots, along with a bottle of cabernet sauvignon. She liked a man who took charge on a date, even though she also enjoyed her independence as a single mother who had succeeded on her own.

The moment she'd opened the front door, Conrad had taken one look at her outfit—a deep red V-necked charmeuse dress with matching ballet flats—and told her how nice she looked. This made Audrey flush and reminded her that there were still men out there who appreciated a well-dressed woman. Likewise, some women could very much appreciate a well-dressed man. Especially one who smelled good, too.

Audrey admired Conrad in his navy blazer, burgundy oxford and khaki twills without making it seem too obvious. She tried to check her thoughts, which bordered on carnal. No reason to get carried away.

Not yet, anyway.

Once the waiter left, Conrad wondered where to begin without giving himself away. *Maybe I should simply tell her who I really am and face the consequences.*

Instead, he decided to tackle the reason Conrad believed she had accepted his invitation. "How difficult or easy will it be to paint me? I know as a photographer some of my subjects can be a challenge to get just right, no matter how much I know about taking pictures."

Audrey studied him, intrigued with the question. She mentally traced the lines in his square-jawed face and the prominent bone structure ending in a chiseled chin. "I think with your features—and your ability to sit still—it won't be difficult at all. Depending, of course, on exactly what you are looking for."

"I suppose what I'd like is something along the lines of the painting you did of Grant Pearson, minus the uniform and helmet."

She cocked a brow.

Conrad detected her hesitation and said nonchalantly, "Is that going to be a problem?"

"No," she stated. "I just think that you'd be much happier with a more classical portrait that focuses on the strengths of your face and character rather than a painting that was done from a photograph absent of the particulars only an actual sitting can capture."

Conrad could hardly object. He also didn't wish to make her suspicious of his motives. "Well, you're the artist and know what's best."

"And you're the subject and I want you to be happy."

He smiled. "I will be happy knowing you're painting me and giving me a taste of immortality."

Audrey sipped her wine and decided this might be a good time to ask something that had been on her mind. "So who is this painting for, anyway?" She tried to make the question sound as blasé as possible, but felt it was reasonable, all things considered. "Do you have a girlfriend back in Charleston you've failed to mention?" He did say he was divorced.

A boyish grin formed on one side of Conrad's mouth. "There's no one in my life at the moment. The painting is for my mother."

Your mother, of course. Paintings make perfect gifts for mothers.

"How nice." For some reason Audrey felt relieved, but still curious. "Does your mother live in Charleston?"

"Yes, along with my stepfather." Conrad waited a moment. "I'm sorry about your parents."

Audrey hesitated, wondering if she wanted to go there. "Thank you," she said sadly. She could see sadness and sincerity in his eyes, as though he could relate. Maybe he could. Somehow she felt like sharing more of herself with him and hoped Conrad returned the favor.

"It's been so long, yet sometimes it seems like it was just yesterday," she reflected.

The waiter came with their food and Conrad contemplated revealing everything. He could read Audrey's thoughts because they were very much his own. She had lost something that could never be replaced and it had impacted her entire life in so many ways.

After the waiter moved on, Conrad followed up where Audrey left off. "You mentioned that the firefighter, Grant Pearson, saved your life during this fire?"

"Yes." Audrey stiffened. "He seemed to come from nowhere, as if God Almighty had sent him inside our house and into my room, where the thick smoke was suffocating. I remember clinging to him. When I first woke up and I realized the house was on fire, I prayed that my family would get out alive. He succeeded on part of that prayer and was valiant in trying to save my parents…"

"Did he say anything to you?" Conrad asked and hoped the question seemed a natural one, under the circumstances. "I mean, I can only imagine the stress and strain you were both under. I wondered if he might've somehow known what would happen to him if he went back in that house."

"He just told me to be calm and everything would be all right." Audrey picked through her carrots as if in a daze. "I'm sure he believed that. I wanted to with all my heart. When Grant handed me to someone outside, I begged him not to let my parents die. He said he wouldn't and that God was with them." She choked back the words. "It was the last time I saw Grant Pearson alive, other than the hazy images in my mind that won't go away. And I never saw my parents again. And those images… I'm not even sure I want them to go away, since they're all I have left of…"

It was all Conrad could do not to shed tears as he watched them well in Audrey's eyes. His father believed in what he was doing and that God would protect him and those he tried to rescue.

Audrey could see that Conrad was genuinely moved by her experience. This, too, was something she hadn't seen in other men. They usually did not want to hear about such terrible things, as if they would somehow be contagious. Conrad really was different. She only wished he didn't live so far away.

Audrey thought about the day she saw him at the cemetery. The gravesite he went to was not far from Grant Pearson's grave. Who was the family friend Conrad spoke of? Did he have any kin in Festive Cove?

She met his gaze. "So was the person you visited at the cemetery someone you were really close to or…?"

Conrad knew this was coming. It was only a matter of time before curiosity got the better of Audrey, considering that she saw him standing over a headstone, just feet away from his father's gravesite. Why hadn't he come right out with it from the very start? Now it was too late to go back. If he said the wrong thing it would be a disaster. To say the right thing would perhaps be even worse at this stage.

"I actually never knew the lady."

"I don't understand…." Audrey raised a brow.

Conrad sighed and said what amounted to a half-truth, "My mother used to live in Festive Cove. She wanted me to be sure to drop by the cemetery to visit one of her best friends who died young." He tried to convince himself that he wasn't really lying—his parents were best friends, in fact, always giving each other a shoulder to cry on if need be.

Conrad watched as Audrey pondered his explanation. Finally her eyes softened into what seemed to be quiet acceptance. He hoped the subject never came up again. He didn't want to hurt her.

Conrad was beginning to believe there was not much more to be gained by looking back. On the other hand, there was much to be gained by looking forward. He couldn't help eyeing the attractive lady in a whole new light....

They had cheesecake for dessert along with coffee. Audrey was amazed that Conrad's mother had actually lived in Festive Cove.

"When did your mother move away?" She looked at him while putting the cup to her mouth.

"A long time ago," Conrad said simply.

Audrey imagined they could have crossed paths, considering it was a relatively small town. As their mothers were probably around the same age, they might have been good friends.

Conrad and I might have had years to make a connection instead of days.

"And your father?"

Conrad stared at the question, wanting to spill the beans about his relationship to the man she knew as Grant Pearson. But this wasn't the time or place, though he wasn't quite sure when or where that would be. *Soon,* he promised himself, *when the time is right...*

"He died."

"I'm sorry."

"It happened when I was pretty young." Conrad looked away. "My mother has since remarried." But no one could ever take the place of his real father.

Audrey sliced into a piece of cheesecake and put it in her mouth as Conrad followed suit. She found herself growing more comfortable with this man than she would have thought possible after such a short time. Her defense mechanisms against being hurt again were always lurking, but so far the warning bells seemed to have faded into the background.

"Do you have a portfolio?" she asked him. "I'd really love to see some of your work."

Conrad wiped crumbs form his lips with a napkin. "I didn't bring my portfolio with me, but I'd be more than happy to show you photographs. You can always check my Web site." He gave her the URL.

"Wonderful." Audrey smiled. She had known a couple of photographers over the years, but never taken a personal interest in their work. It always felt good to explore a fellow artist's expression.

Conrad again wished he could be more forthcoming with Audrey. He feared it would be a mistake to say more than he could probably handle sharing right now. Thankfully there was his love for photography to discuss, along with her passion for art.

"Maybe I could photograph you sometime, Audrey?" Conrad said on the spur of the moment, wondering why he hadn't thought of it sooner. "And Stacy, too."

"Maybe," Audrey said, though never entirely at ease with having her picture taken. No such worries for her daughter. "Stacy loves to be in front of the camera every chance she gets. She's a total ham."

"Good for her. She's a beautiful girl, much like her mother. That usually translates into excellent pictures."

"Well, thanks for the compliment. I'll try not to get too bigheaded from it."

Audrey blushed, even as Conrad could tell she was very much down to earth where it concerned her looks. Indeed, he doubted that Audrey even realized just how attractive she was.

Conrad was curious as to why Audrey didn't have a man in her life. Had she sworn off men due to bad experiences? Perhaps she was a workaholic like him, at the expense of a serious and committed relationship.

"So why no man in your life?" he asked casually. "Or do your work and Stacy pretty much make dating something that's low on the totem pole?"

Audrey tilted her head. "No, it's not about my work or raising a daughter, even if both can be a handful at times. I was married once briefly and regrettably, aside from the child we brought into the world. Unfortunately, I've found that most men I've dated have been too much into themselves or dishonest or both. I don't need that in my life."

"Surely you don't believe all men are like that?" He eyed her unblinkingly.

"No, not every man." She offered him a soft smile. "Not you, I think."

"Nice to hear."

Conrad drank coffee and felt more than a little guilty about his own dishonesty. But he refused to lump himself into the same category as those men. For one, he wasn't exactly dating her in the true sense of the word. Certainly not under false pretenses in relation to his availability or character. He knew the truth would come out sooner or later—he just hoped Audrey would be understanding and forgiving.

"Where does Stacy's father fit into the scheme of things?" Conrad hoped he wasn't overstepping any bounds.

Audrey frowned. "He doesn't and hasn't for a very long time. We were two people who never should have gotten together, but had to learn the hard way."

"Yeah, sounds like me and my ex." He became pensive. "Thought we had the right stuff to make it work. Couldn't have been further from the truth."

"Did either of you want kids or did that not have anything to do with the breakup?" she asked curiously.

Somehow it struck Audrey that Conrad would make a wonderful father. Or was she way off base there?

Conrad looked at her face. "I suppose it had something to do with our marriage ending. I lost my own father early in life and so, in that sense, wasn't in much of a hurry to have kids. My ex-wife moved back and forth on this issue, but never seemed committed enough to want a family. By the time we both began to think differently about the issue, we had grown too far apart to keep the marriage alive."

Audrey felt badly for Conrad that he, too, had experienced the anguish of losing a parent during childhood. Obviously this had affected his own life and his prospects for fatherhood. She was sorry, too, for the ex-wife who lost a good man in Conrad, even if they weren't meant to stay together. But life was all about twists and turns that were not always understood till later—if ever. Audrey was certain that his past misfortunes and mistakes would turn into a greater understanding and positive experiences in the future.

The glass-half-full approach is the way I try to deal with my own tragedies and poor choices, and overall it seems to be working.

She lifted her cup on that note, feeling courageous. "Well, in the spirit of the season, let's hope that the holidays and beyond bring good tidings to us both."

Conrad favored her with a brilliant smile, holding up his cup. He wanted the same more than anything. Especially if such tidings could involve her in his life.

"I'll definitely drink to that, Audrey."

Chapter 10

Conrad walked Audrey to her front door. He hoped she would ask him in for coffee and more conversation, not really wanting the evening to end. It had been a while since he had so enjoyed the company of a woman. He was still trying to come to grips with the fact this particular eye-catching and talented lady was the same skinny seven-year-old he knew in another life.

I wonder what kissing her will feel like? No doubt, spine-tingling.

Instincts told Conrad that Audrey wanted to kiss him, too.

Gazing at Audrey, he angled his face and kissed

her mouth softly but unwaveringly. She kissed him back and seemed to enjoy the kiss every bit as much as he did. He went to deepen it.

It was Audrey who pulled back. "That was nice."

"Very nice." Conrad could actually remember her taste, slightly sweet and a little tart.

"Thanks for a lovely evening, Conrad."

He smiled. "It was my pleasure. I hope we can do it again soon."

"I'd like that." She looked up at him. "Well, I'd better go check on my daughter."

"Good night, Audrey," Conrad said, hiding his disappointment because he truly respected the love Audrey had for Stacy. After all, his own memories of childhood were all about such love and caring.

But Conrad could now admit that this moment wasn't about the past. He wanted the woman, right here and now, for herself.

"So I'll see you this weekend, then, for the first sitting?" Audrey voiced, knowing that starting Conrad's portrait would mean delaying other projects but not minding the delays in the least.

"I'll be here," he promised.

She watched Conrad walk back to his vehicle and touched her lips, still feeling the tingle of his mouth on hers.

Audrey waved once more as he drove off into the darkness, brightened by flashing Christmas lights from neighboring houses.

She had wanted to invite him in but had decided against it. For a very good reason.

I like Conrad, I really do. He seems like the complete package with all the qualities I'm looking for in a man, including being a great kisser. And Stacy likes him.

But should I allow myself to get too close to someone who probably won't even be in town by January first?

She definitely wasn't into one-nighters, even if one night with Conrad promised to be truly out of this world.

Audrey didn't believe it was really practical to think about a relationship. And would anything less be fair to her, him or her daughter?

The following morning, Conrad was awakened by the doorbell. He could have used another hour of shut-eye, but someone obviously thought otherwise. He quickly threw on some clothes and headed downstairs.

"All right, all right, I'm coming," he groaned, crossing the hallway into the foyer.

Conrad raised a brow when he opened the door and saw Willis standing there. Only he wasn't alone. In hand was a dog.

"Hey, there." Willis grinned.

"Hey, Willis." Conrad eyed the cocker spaniel.

"The other night you said you were feeling a little lonely here, being away from your friends and family for the holiday. So I thought you might be able to use some company while you're in town."

"Did you?"

"Yeah." He laughed. "So here's your new holiday family."

Conrad furrowed his brow. *I'd love to have someone to hold. But a dog wasn't exactly what I had in mind.* He reluctantly showed Willis in.

"This is Mars," said Willis, petting the dog. "One of the firefighters decided the Bahamas was a better place to live. He left behind his cute little cocker spaniel. The laws for importing a dog are unreasonable, and spending months in quarantine seemed cruel. Mars has been the unofficial fire-department mascot for a couple of weeks now. Unfortunately he's been banished by the chief who is allergic to him. I tried to take him home, but my wife felt that having three dogs was more than she could handle. So here I am, hoping in this Christmas season you'll take pity on Mars. Otherwise it's the animal shelter—or worse. Which *nobody* wants."

Conrad's first thought was to pass on being a dog sitter, fearing that it would be too much hassle when his focus was elsewhere. But the more he played with the dog, the more he took a liking to him.

"Is he house trained?" Conrad didn't need any accidents in his borrowed domain.

Willis nodded. "The dog knows when and where

to do his business and behave himself. He won't give you any trouble, I promise. You can count on a good and loyal friend for as long as you'll have him."

"I can see that," Conrad said, as Mars seemed to have all but forgotten his previous owner. He hopped up on Conrad's leg as he knelt down to pet the dog's head. Compassion took over. "Looks like you've got yourself a new temporary home, boy."

The dog barked its approval. Conrad would not even rule out bringing Mars back to Charleston if they really got along great.

Willis put a hand on Conrad's shoulder. "Well, I'll just leave you two to get acquainted while I go to work. Hopefully I won't have to put out any fires today."

"That goes doubly for me," Conrad said thoughtfully, not wishing the worst on anyone.

An hour later, Conrad rang Jayne. "I need you to zip me a selection of some of my best photos," he told her, thinking of Audrey's request. "Stuff not up on the Web site."

"Will do. You plan to open up a Washington branch of Pearson Quality Photography Studio?"

Conrad laughed. "I don't think so, though you never know. I have a potential client who would like to see samples of what I can do with the camera."

"You mean, you can't convince this would-be client with your charm alone?" she teased.

"Perhaps, but as they say, the proof is in the picture." Conrad paused thoughtfully. "In fact, scratch that idea. Just put together a real portfolio for me and overnight it. That would be a much more effective way of demonstrating my talents."

And another means in which he could sell himself as both a photographer and down-to-earth person to Audrey. *I'd love to photograph her, day and night. She'd make a great subject.*

"I'll get right to work on that," Jayne promised. "Anything else, boss?"

"Just keep smiling and stay on your toes," he said.

"Same to you."

After hanging up, Conrad speed dialed Audrey's number. He got her voice mail, but shook off the disappointment in not speaking to her live.

"Hello, Audrey, it's Conrad. Just called to say again how much I enjoyed spending time with you last night. I'm looking forward to sitting for the portrait. It'll be a first for me. Hope I can stay still long enough to get it right. Talk to you soon. Bye."

Conrad wondered if it was a mistake to attach too much significance to a kiss. Maybe he was setting himself up for a fall.

Or maybe this could be the most wonderful thing to happen to them both, even if there were still some obstacles to get past.

He went to play with Mars, though Audrey was still very much on Conrad's mind.

* * *

Audrey took measured breaths as she lay on her back, legs raised slightly, during the Pilates mat classes at the Healthy Body Day Spa. Beside her was Regina, who had introduced her to the Pilates body-conditioning program.

"So when do I get to meet Mr. *Ultra* Handsome and *Sexy* Photographer?" Regina asked.

Now that's a good question. Audrey was still enjoying the aftereffects of the kiss three days ago, but refused to put too much into it. Or start making plans for Conrad to meet her friends. Not just yet.

First I'd like to get to know the man better myself.

She brought her knees up to her chest in a relaxing motion. "Soon," was all Audrey could promise.

Regina frowned. "Well, don't wait till he's back in Charleston. Otherwise I'll never speak to you again."

Audrey laughed softly. "I'm sure it won't have to come to that. Conrad will at least be in town till after I've completed his portrait, which will take more than one sitting." She considered that he could leave and come back. The thought was somehow disheartening to Audrey. Conrad was not her man and she certainly had no claim to keep him in Festive Cove any longer than his business called for.

"In that case, you definitely won't be able to keep him all to yourself, girl."

"I wouldn't dream of it, Regina." *Good thing*

*you're already spoken for. Otherwise we just might
be in a heated competition for Conrad.*

Two hours later Audrey taught her art class at
Festive Cove's community college. It was a way of
giving something back to the town that gave her so
much in the way of kindness and support after the
death of her parents. She also fancied the idea of
contributing to the talents of up-and-coming artists,
any of whom could become the next Van Gogh, Da
Vinci or even, dare she say it, *Lamour.*

That afternoon, Audrey picked up Stacy from
school. She could tell right away that her daughter
was not her usual self.

"What is it, honey?"

"Nothing," she muttered, and stared out the window.

Audrey tried to coax it out of her, knowing that it
could be any of a million things. "Did someone do
something to you at school?"

"No."

"Are you feeling ill?"

"Yeah, but not because I'm sick."

Audrey glanced at her in the rearview mirror and
back to the road, perplexed. "Then why?"

It took a moment or two before Stacy spoke with
sadness in her voice. "Because I wish I had a real daddy
like all my friends, not one who never cared about me."

Audrey furrowed her forehead. "Where did this
come from?"

Stacy pouted. "Everyone likes talking about their daddies. It makes me feel stupid because I can't."

"Oh, sweetheart." Audrey sighed, hating that Julius had turned out to be such an asshole who didn't deserve to have a beautiful and brilliant daughter like Stacy. "Many kids don't have fathers for different reasons. I was your age when I lost my daddy and it was devastating. I know it's hard for you, honey, but you will be okay, too. And you're *not* stupid."

"I know," Stacy spoke tonelessly.

"So when your friends talk about their dads, you talk about *your* mom. Then they'll have to talk about their moms and be just as proud of them."

Stacy managed a giggle.

"Is that a *not*-proud-of-*your*-mom giggle?" teased Audrey.

"No. I am very proud of you, Mommy!"

"Well, that's a relief. And I'm very proud of you, sweetheart. I always will be. You're very, very loved. Even if you only have a mommy around."

Audrey wondered if she should be worried. She hadn't wanted her daughter to grow up without a father. But neither Audrey nor Stacy had a choice in the matter.

Julius made that choice. What an unfortunate loss for him.

Audrey considered that a stepfather to love and cherish Stacy, hopefully making her forget all about

her real daddy, was always a possibility. For some
reason, Conrad's face popped into Audrey's head as
a potential candidate.

Chapter 11

On Saturday, the snow came down like fluffy pieces of cotton, settling on the landscape as if they had nowhere better to go. Audrey let Stacy talk her into building a snowman as a prelude to putting up the outside Christmas lights. It was a ritual Audrey had avoided for years because of the memories it evoked. But now that Stacy was old enough to appreciate the spirit of Christmas and the joy of decorations, Audrey managed to put aside past haunts and do the right thing for her daughter.

By the time they finished the snowman, it was crooked and uneven, but somehow still standing. Then Stacy caught Audrey flush on the shoulder with a snowball, giggling when it made impact.

Once she recovered from the shock, Audrey laughed. "So that's the way you want to play it, huh, kiddo? Have it your way."

She scooped up some snow, bunched it into a ball and tossed it at her daughter, missing badly.

Stacy chuckled and grabbed more snow, flinging it. Soon they were in a full-scale, old-fashioned snowball fight, the likes of which Audrey had not seen since she was a child. She had forgotten how much fun it could be.

At one point Audrey threw a snowball at Stacy. Only it sailed high over her head and crashed against the chest of Conrad. He looked taken aback, sporting a crooked grin.

"Oops, sorry," Audrey uttered with embarrassment. "Didn't see you." In fact, she hadn't expected him for another two hours. Or had she lost track of time while dodging snowballs?

"It's okay. I'm not all that easy to spot at six-five," he joked, wiping off the snow with his leather gloved hand.

Audrey blushed and glanced to where Conrad had parked at the curb. She was surprised they hadn't heard him drive up. Gazing at Conrad, Audrey couldn't help but remember their kiss and how it made her feel.

Was it still on his mind, too?

Audrey jumped when Stacy caught her in the stomach with another snowball. She faced her giggling daughter and said, "You're going to get it, Ms. Snowballer. But another time."

"Oh, don't let me stop the fun," Conrad said with amusement, enjoying this playful side of her. He was tempted to join in.

"Be careful what you ask for," warned Audrey, threatening to grab more snow to throw at him.

He laughed and pretended to brace himself for impact.

She grinned. "Aren't you a bit early for the sitting?"

"Guilty as charged," he admitted. "I didn't have anything better to do this afternoon, so thought I'd take a chance and come ahead of schedule."

And give myself more time to spend with you and Stacy.

"Well, your mistake," Audrey indicated mischievously. "Stacy and I were just about to string up some Christmas lights. And since you're here, you can help."

Conrad's brow furrowed good-humoredly, then he turned toward the house. He could imagine it being transformed into a holiday paradise and the idea excited him for some reason. Once he looked at Audrey's beautiful face, her eyes regarding him tentatively, he knew exactly what that reason was.

"It would be my pleasure," he said truthfully, only too happy to assist her in any way she liked.

Stacy grabbed his hand and said spiritedly, "C'mon, I'll show you where the lights are."

Conrad flashed a whimsical smile at Audrey and allowed the girl to pull him toward the house.

Two hours later the lights and wreath were up and the house looked to Conrad like a Christmas card brought to life. It brought him back to the days when it was a very big deal for the family to decorate the house, inside and out. His parents were always in the spirit and wanted him to be, too. That was less the case during Conrad's marriage, when neither he nor his ex had been able to muster up the enthusiasm to go all-out for the holidays. The joy of Christmas and family had been missing in his life for a long, long time and he wondered if it was too late to recapture the magic.

Conrad grabbed his camera from his car and snapped a couple of pictures of the house, then a few more of Audrey and Stacy in front of it. Both seemed natural as subjects and were easy to photograph. He managed to coax them into another snowball fight, capturing mother and daughter on film. He planned to give the pictures to them for Christmas and take more professional photos later, if given the chance.

Audrey had relented to being photographed, trusting Conrad that she wouldn't come across as too this or too that, but just right in her own mind. The fact that Stacy had sided with Conrad made it difficult for Audrey to say no—even if she'd much rather paint the faces of others or perhaps take her own turn behind the camera.

In the end it seemed the least Audrey could do after Conrad had generously given of his time to help put up the lights on a cold, snowy day. It would have been a much harder task without him.

Now it was Audrey's turn to be the creative one and she felt right in her element. Conrad sat in her studio looking not quite at her as instructed. She sensed that he was slightly uncomfortable, as most subjects usually were in the beginning. It was her job to make him feel relaxed, so she could capture his spirit and make sure the painting never lost any of its vitality.

"Tell me what you do for fun in Charleston, Conrad?" Audrey was standing in front of the canvas, painting delicate strokes, sizing up her subject.

"What don't I do is probably more like it." He gave a low chuckle. "Honestly, I'm too busy to have much fun these days. But when I do find some time, I like to run, read, play tennis, softball, bowl, dance, swim and take my boat out during the summer."

"You have a boat?"

"Yep."

She fluttered her lashes. "I'm impressed."

"Don't be. It's a ten-year-old thirty-foot sailboat that gives me fits at times. One day I hope to trade it in for something really nice."

"I have to confess that I don't know anything about sailing," Audrey stated, picturing him in sexy sailor's clothing while maneuvering his boat expertly in the waters.

"Not much to it. A little instruction and time out on the water and you'll have the fish eating out of your hands in no time. And probably me, too."

Audrey laughed, loving his sense of humor. Most men she met seemed far too serious for their own good. Except when they were sweet talking someone to get what they wanted. It was nice to meet someone who appeared to have a likable balance to his character.

She studied Conrad's face and tried to familiarize herself with every detail. There was a gentle quality about his look that came through despite the hard lines around his mouth and on his brow, as if he had weathered a few storms in his day. She wondered about Conrad's life over the years.

Was it mostly a happy one? He had lost a parent at a young age, too. This had obviously had an effect on his marriage and his desire to have children. But it hadn't prevented him from pursuing his passion for photography. Perhaps, much as she had, he'd used tragedy as a motivating force.

Conrad stole a glance at Audrey every chance he got. He could see that she was a study in concentration, intent on getting every nuance of his image as though anything less would be unacceptable. If only he could read her mind, find out what went on in it while she was practicing her craft.

His own state of mind was admittedly on a different plane than when he first came to Festive Cove. He had wanted to feel animosity toward the woman who lived today while his father had been dead for more than two decades. Hadn't his anger and grief been the thing that'd been driving him all these years? But he just didn't feel those emotions when he was around her.

Audrey was a decent woman and more appealing than he could have imagined. He hadn't come to town looking for romance. But feelings were developing between them and there was no denying it. Their kiss seemed to rule out any thoughts that it was just his imagination.

Conrad only wished he could tell Audrey now that their paths had crossed long ago, before either of them had a clue as to what life and loss was truly about. But to do so would risk everything that they seemed to be establishing. Still, deep down he knew that the deeper this got, the harder it would be to go down that path....

Turing the pages of Conrad's portfolio as they sat in the living room, Audrey was impressed with the man's photographic abilities. He was really good. She imagined he could make anyone look great on film.

"How long have you been doing this?" She regarded Conrad's handsome profile.

"Oh, since I was about eight or nine," he answered, thinking back to his first real camera.

"So it's been in your blood for the better part of your life?"

"You could say that." Photography had been the one constant when things were difficult—something Conrad could count on to keep his head above water. "I'm almost a different person behind the camera."

Audrey widened her eyes at him. "I think I know what you mean."

"I'm sure you do," he said with a nod, watching as she lifted a mug of coffee and took a sip.

"I guess most creative people are so focused on their craft that it can be an almost out-of-body experience when working."

Conrad concurred. "Yeah, tell me about it." He paused thoughtfully. "So when did you first know you wanted to be an artist?" *Could it have actually been around the same time I knew photography was in my blood?* He was interested in knowing more and more about her, professionally and otherwise.

Audrey stared at the question. *When did I?* She recalled the first paintbrushes her parents had given her at age five or six. Had she known instinctively even then that this would be her life's work?

She met Conrad's gaze and said, "I think I probably knew at an early age, but didn't really take it seriously till I went to art school in New York City."

Conrad remembered reading a bit about her art

education as part of Audrey's bio in the magazine. "The Big Apple must have been an experience after growing up in a small town like this." He should know. While Charleston was hardly New York, it was a leap from Festive Cove in population and diversity.

"Yes, it was different, but in a good way. Living in New York, and later Paris and Johannesburg for a bit, helped prepare me for the classic art of portraiture. So many faces to digest and use to better understand bone structure, skin shades, different looks and expressions. It also helped me as a single woman trying to make my way in the highly competitive and not always easy art world."

"Looks like the end has definitely justified the means." Conrad eyed her approvingly.

Audrey's lips curved into a smile. "Well, I'd like to think that it's still somewhere in the middle for me. I've come a long way, but still have a long way to go as an artist, mother and woman." And maybe even a wife again.

"I'd say you've got it going in all three categories," he told her candidly.

"Why thank you, Conrad," she said sweetly. "I'm not used to so many compliments all at once."

"Well, you should be. I haven't said anything that I don't believe is true." *Even though I haven't been entirely truthful with you. And for that I'm sorry.*

Audrey was touched to the point of being speechless. Men like Conrad simply didn't come into her

life every day, if ever. She wished he lived in Festive
Cove or any of the nearby cities and towns, instead
of being there on borrowed time.

"Thanks for agreeing to paint me," he said. "I
think it'll mean a lot to my mother."

"Thanks for choosing me as your artist," Audrey
tossed back at him. "And it's a pleasure being able
to put your handsome face on canvas." Not to mention embedded in her mind, where she could admire
him anytime she wanted.

"You flatter me." Conrad grinned. "I'll look forward to seeing the finished product."

"I hope you like it," Audrey said hesitantly. There
were few dissatisfied clients. But somehow it was especially important that he accept wholeheartedly her
interpretation of him. It was almost as though she
had begun this painting long ago, if only in her mind,
and come full circle in wanting to complete the
project satisfactorily.

"How could I not?" Conrad gave her a straight look.
"Especially when I've become so fond of the artist."

"Oh, *really?*"

"Yes, really." He swallowed and zeroed in on her
mouth, which looked mighty appetizing.

Audrey could tell that he wanted to kiss her again.
She wanted him to. It was as if the first time had
merely been a prelude to a hunger building inside
with a passion that would only grow until their lips
touched again.

Conrad did not disappoint. Sensing that they were on the same wavelength, he leaned his head ever so slightly and put his mouth upon hers. The kiss seemed to last forever and had his heart beating a thousand times a minute. Audrey's heart seemed to be racing just as fast and he could feel a slight quiver in her soft, full lips. Suddenly they embraced one another as if to find something useful to do with their hands and arms, and enjoyed the moment like it was pure magic.

Audrey lost herself in the openmouthed kiss. Time and space seemed to stand still. It had been too long since a kiss had swept her away like that. Did Conrad feel the same way?

When they pulled away from each other, Conrad felt it was time for him to leave. Restraint had never been one of his finer points. But it was the right thing to do. He didn't want anything to spoil this. And he certainly didn't want to rush into something that deserved to be approached slowly but surely—indicating he truly cared for her beyond a quick need for release.

"I should be going," he said huskily.

Audrey thought about asking Conrad to stay, wanting more of what she'd just experienced and beyond. Clearly he was a man used to taking his sweet time in romancing a woman and she could respect that.

"Yes, I guess I'd better check in on Stacy."

He smiled. "Can I call you tomorrow?"

"Please do."

"Count on it."

Conrad gave Audrey one more kiss at the door. It was less intense but every bit as potent in telling that he wanted her. The way she responded told him the feeling was mutual.

On the drive home, Conrad reeled from the realization that something powerful was occurring between him and Audrey. He could feel it in his bones. It excited and scared him at once. He had no idea what this meant for either of them in the future. Could they actually have a long-distance relationship? Could they get past their devastating history?

Chapter 12

Audrey tucked Stacy into bed, pulling the appliquéd trapunto quilt to just under her chin and studying her as though a work of art. Stacy turned over in her sleep and was snoring softly. It had been a while since Conrad had left and Audrey wondered just where this was headed, if anywhere at all. Yes, they were becoming romantic in their time together, with her knees growing weak whenever they kissed. But was that the same thing as beginning a relationship? Could she afford to let her guard down and risk getting hurt by a man again?

She wanted romance, but she didn't want to get her hopes up that Conrad might be someone who could make her happy, only for it all to come crashing down with a thud. Then there was her daughter to think about. Conrad certainly seemed to like Stacy and she liked him, which was equally important. But was there room in his life for both of them? And could a long-distance relationship work between two people who were clearly carrying scars from the past?

Audrey kissed Stacy on the cheek and left the room, closing the door quietly so as not to wake her. She went to her room down the hall and slipped into the Biedermeier-style bed, wrapping herself with a jacquard-stitch duvet cover. A sliver of moonlight came in through the heavily pleated draperies. After adjusting to the moonlight, Audrey scanned the master suite as if for the first time. She could make out the antique double dresser with a mirror and stool and the retro armoire. She saw the plush loveseat, square glass table and television. There were hanging ivy and fern plants in every corner and the walls contained framed original artwork given to her by fellow artists.

Drifting off to sleep, Audrey found herself going back in time to when she was seven years old. It was the wee hours of Christmas morning and a fire had broken out in the house. She was trapped and fearful of being burned alive. Just when it seemed like all hope was lost, the fireman came to her rescue. She was safe.

But where were her parents? Someone had to save them from the terrible flames....

* * *

Audrey awoke with a start to the sound of her own wail. She felt oddly cold beneath the warm cover.

She realized that Stacy was standing there in her nightgown as if lost. Audrey feared that her daughter had been frightened awake by the moaning.

"What is it, honey?" Audrey asked self-consciously.

"I just felt weird," Stacy uttered, rubbing her eyes. "Can I sleep with you tonight?"

"Of course you can, baby." Audrey gave a silent thank-you that she had apparently not been the source of this unrest. She pulled the cover back and invited Stacy in, cuddling her.

"Are you always going to be here, Mommy? Or will you leave like Daddy did?"

Audrey choked back tears. "Oh, honey, I will never, ever abandon you."

"Promise?"

"I promise with all my heart." *How can I really promise that?* What if she were taken away by forces beyond her control like her own parents? Audrey could only hope to always be there for Stacy and pray that God was listening.

"Do you like Conrad?" Stacy asked, her voice brimming with curiosity.

The question caught Audrey off guard. "Yes, I like him."

"A lot?"

"Well, I really don't know Conrad all that well to like him too much yet, honey," she spoke truthfully. "I do feel that he's a nice man."

"Do you think he likes me?"

"I think he does. What do you think?"

Stacy paused. "I think so. But do you think he ever wants kids? Or a daughter someday?"

Audrey pondered this. She wasn't sure if Conrad could ever get past the issues with his own father leaving him prematurely to ever become one. Much less become the father of someone else's child. But maybe she had him pegged wrong. Maybe he just needed to find the right woman. And right child.

Still, the last thing Audrey wanted was to give Stacy false hope that Conrad would one day become the father she'd never had.

Or the husband Audrey wanted to love and always be there for her and Stacy.

"I'm not really sure Conrad knows what he wants, Stacy," she told her. Or who. "Maybe he'll let us in on it when he feels like talking."

Until then, Audrey was determined not to take anything for granted and continue to live the life she was given.

If only for the sake of her daughter.

Chapter 13

"Hello, Momma," Conrad said on his cell phone while driving, having expected her call.

"Is everything all right?"

"I'm fine."

"I take it you've spoken with Audrey Beaumont?"

"I have, and it's now Audrey Lamour."

"Well, she's a sweet woman. I hope you didn't make her feel any worse than she probably already does with what happened that Christmas morning."

Conrad couldn't help but smile, knowing that his mother had believed this to be a foolhardy expedition. He didn't necessarily agree, even if his line of reasoning had since become blurred. His original in-

tentions for returning to Festive Cove had fallen by
the wayside, replaced with the utmost respect for
Audrey Lamour and an intense attraction that he
never anticipated.

*The fact that she doesn't know my true identity is
beside the point. She's a terrific woman who I wish
I'd gotten to know better over the years. It's my own
fault for not doing the right thing when she reached
out in the first place.*

"It was never about Audrey, per se," he suggested, "but Dad. She told me what she could. I
didn't ask for more."

"And was that enough to quell your need to know?"

"I think I have a better understanding about what
Dad went through and why. Audrey suffered every
bit as much as I did, probably more considering what
she lost, and I don't want to see her hurting anymore.
Quite the contrary, I want only the best for Audrey
and her little girl."

"Well, your father would be very happy to know
that, Ulysses. He rescued Audrey for a reason. Maybe it was for his son to better appreciate the sacrifice
he made and the selflessness of his efforts."

Conrad mused regretfully. He never wanted to be
bitter toward his father. Or the Beaumonts. Especially Audrey. It just seemed to be his only option for
the longest time. Feeling sorry for himself for being
fatherless made everything else in Conrad's life
almost an afterthought.

He now accepted that his father only did what the job called for, with a bravery Conrad envied.

"I think you're right, Momma," he said.

"I know I am. If going back to Festive Cove was what it took to get you to put things in a proper perspective, then I couldn't be happier."

"Neither could I." *And for more reasons than you could possibly realize.*

Conrad stood in the Christmas-tree lot. After spending time with Audrey and Stacy yesterday and helping decorate their house, he felt fresh inspiration to put up a tree in Lucille's house. It would help liven up the house. He walked around and could see that the best trees had already been taken. Maybe this was a bad idea? Could be far more trouble than it was worth. He hadn't put up a Christmas tree since his divorce, feeling there was no point.

He saw one that looked as if it would be a good fit in the living room. It was identified as a Fraser fir and was nearly seven feet tall with bushy branches.

"A real beaut, ain't she?" the aging attendant said.

"Yeah, it is."

"One of the last good ones left."

"I can see that," Conrad said.

"You want to take it with you?"

"I was just thinking that I might."

Ten minutes later, Conrad had tied the tree to the roof of his Range Rover, purchased lights, ornaments and tinsel at the store down the street and was on his way.

During the drive home, Conrad conceded that he really liked Audrey, over and beyond the physical attraction and sexual appeal. Both had come a long ways from when they were kids. She had the type of courage lacking in most women he'd dated in the past. And her talents, impressive as they were, made Audrey all the more appealing.

And because of her own losses, she seemed to understand him.

But was it possible for them to have a serious long-distance relationship? Could they get past their shared history at the end of the day?

We're both adults now and if Audrey and I are truly on the same wavelength, we can find a way to deal with any thorny issues that may come between us and somehow make this work.

Conrad pulled into the driveway. It would not be easy telling Audrey that they knew each other once upon a time at this point. On the other hand, the closer they grew to each other, the more difficult it was to spoil the festive holiday spirit and risk putting what they seemed to have in jeopardy.

He dragged the tree across the snow-packed driveway, leaving it at the side of the house for now. Maybe he would invite Audrey and Stacy over to help him decorate it. That could be fun and an opportunity for further bonding.

* * *

After making himself hot chocolate, Conrad put his plan into action, phoning Audrey.

"Hi, Conrad." Her voice, sweet and mellow, was growing on him and he loved hearing it.

"I decided the house I'm staying in needed to be more cheery, so I bought a Christmas tree."

"How nice."

"I was hoping that maybe this evening you and Stacy could come by and we could turn my tree into a masterpiece, much like yours."

"I'd love to," Audrey said with enthusiasm. "Unfortunately I have choir rehearsal tonight, Conrad."

He could tell that she regretted this. So did Conrad. Perhaps had he still been a regular churchgoer, he would be able to better appreciate the uplifting spirit that often came with singing hymns.

Audrey continued to amaze him with her talents. "I didn't know you sang in the choir."

"Been doing it for a few years now. My momma used to sing in the choir. I'm not nearly as good as she was, but I guess I can blend in without too many people noticing if I'm a bit off-key."

Conrad was sure she was just being modest, as with her artwork. This was another very attractive quality the lady had about her.

"If you can hold off decorating the tree till tomorrow night, Stacy and I would be happy to join in," Audrey offered.

Conrad smiled. "Oh, I can definitely hold off till then."

"So we have ourselves a date."

He liked the sound of that, even if it fell a bit short of what Conrad considered a "real date." Then again, any time spent in Audrey's presence was better than just about any other date he'd had.

"Yeah, we do," he responded happily.

"Good. Stacy has some leftover handmade ornaments that I'm sure she would be delighted to hang on your tree, if you like."

"That would be a nice touch."

He gave her the address, already looking forward to the company.

Conrad brought the tree in out of the cold, giving it time to thaw before the big day.

Chapter 14

Audrey liked the idea of visiting Conrad's house in the no-pressure, fun event of decorating his Christmas tree. It also gave her the chance to see how he and Stacy got along in his own environment. In the past this had sometimes proven to be disastrous, as Stacy's natural curiosity and youthful spirit had been more than some men could handle. Would Conrad be different?

It will be interesting to find out, Audrey thought during the drive across town. So far, Conrad seemed to like her and Stacy, and they liked him. She wouldn't draw too much into that or what the future might hold. If it were meant to be, there would be more to look forward to. If not, she still had been commissioned by Conrad to paint his portrait. And had found a new friend, at the very least.

"Do you think Conrad will like my ornaments?" Stacy asked eagerly from the backseat.

Audrey glanced at her. "How could he not? He'll love them, honey."

"I hope so!"

Audrey realized just how fragile kids could be about even the simplest things. She sensed that Conrad was somehow able to connect with children— or at least her child. What more could she ask for?

"Are we almost there?" whined Stacy with sudden impatience.

"It won't be long now."

Audrey was still curious as to exactly what business had really brought Conrad to town all the way from Charleston. Was it family business? His photography work? It seemed the more she discovered about the man, the more she wanted to know. Which could be good or bad, depending on what she learned.

Conrad was excited about seeing Audrey and Stacy tonight. To him it wasn't about decorating a tree so much as spending quality time together. This trip to Festive Cove had suddenly become much more than the chance to go down memory lane in search of answers. Now he wanted to explore unknown territory and see if it could lead to some-where special down the line.

He almost felt like a kid at Christmas again.

Holding Mars, Conrad peeked through the wood blinds when he heard the car drive up. It was them.

"Looks like we've got company, boy. Better be on your best behavior, if you want to win them over!"

The dog barked as if he understood perfectly.

Conrad opened the door, welcoming his guests.

"This is Mars," he introduced the cocker spaniel.

"Hi, Mars." Stacy touched his head. The dog licked her hand. "Oh, Mommy, he's so cute!"

"I didn't know you had a dog," Audrey said with surprise. Somehow she didn't picture him as a pet-owner type. What else didn't she know about him?

"Haven't had him very long," Conrad said. "Someone gave him to me rather than an animal shelter. Seemed like a good idea to keep me company while I'm here."

"I agree." *And just how long will that be?*

"This place belongs to an old friend of the family. Let me show you around; then we'll see if my tree can be made to look half as good as yours."

"Sounds like a plan."

The first things Audrey noticed were her landscapes side by side against the peach-colored living room wall. She was touched that Conrad had left them out to look at rather than keeping them packaged up.

As though reading her mind, Conrad said, "The

paintings will go back to South Carolina with me and look even better at my place."

Audrey smiled and tried to imagine his house in Charleston. Was it also an English Tudor? Or perhaps an art deco or Italianate style? A Victorian?

Conrad excused himself and returned carrying a tray of snacks and drinks, setting it on the coffee table while Audrey and Stacy decorated the tree. It had been a long time since he performed this age-old ritual in a family setting. Or at least this seemed like the family he never had as an adult. And it reminded Conrad of the family he lost as a child.

He watched Stacy put her homemade ornaments of cardboard gingerbread cookies, Santa lollipops and paper drops on the tree.

"They're wonderful," he marveled at the young talent, though not at all surprised, considering her mother's creativity.

"Thank you," Stacy said, flashing a bright smile at him.

"No, thank you," Conrad insisted. "And you, Audrey, for bringing Christmas to this house."

"We're glad you invited us!" This was the first time Stacy had helped decorate anyone else's tree and Audrey could tell that her daughter was really getting into it. She suspected that Stacy saw in Conrad what her own father could have been. This concerned Audrey a bit. She wanted her daughter to enjoy the experience without becoming too attached to the man.

A difficult task at best, Audrey thought, considering her own growing feelings toward him.

Half an hour later, Conrad plugged in the lights and watched the Christmas tree glow beautifully. Unable to resist, he got his camera to snap a few pictures of Audrey, Stacy and Mars in front of the tree.

"You have to get in some pictures, too, Conrad," insisted Audrey.

"Yeah," seconded Stacy.

He grinned. "You talked me into it."

Putting the camera atop a tripod, Conrad set the timer and joined the threesome. He put his arm around Audrey for the picture. The gesture felt completely natural and made him wish he didn't have to remove it so soon.

Conrad was still trying to come to terms with the little girl he had known in the past and what he knew of the lady today. Would she be able to bridge the gap once Audrey knew the truth about him?

With Conrad's arm snugly around her, Audrey felt as if they were a real couple and didn't want that feeling to go away. Did Conrad feel the same way? She didn't want to read more into what was between them than there really was.

She watched Stacy run off after Mars and worried that her daughter might get into trouble. "I'd better go after her."

"Oh, she'll be fine," Conrad said confidently, still holding on to Audrey. "Let them play."

She gazed at him. "Are you sure?"

"Positive. Mars and Stacy look as if they really like each other and this house gives them plenty of room to roam. We'll check on them in a bit."

Audrey relaxed, recognizing that there probably was no cause for concern. Stacy, though only seven, knew how to behave responsibly.

Conrad caught a whiff of her perfume. "Mmm, you smell delicious."

"Glad you like it." She offered him a generous smile.

"I've been waiting all day to do something," he said in a low voice.

Audrey batted her lashes. "Oh, really? And what might that be?"

Conrad grinned slyly. "This…"

He lowered his lips onto hers for a kiss. She reciprocated and Conrad pulled closer, holding her while they kissed as if the whole world revolved only around them. In his mind it did, if only for a little while.

Conrad felt the gentle curves of Audrey's body molding with his and could imagine how incredible it would be to make love to her. The mere thought filled him with desire.

Audrey could have kissed him forever, the way Conrad's exquisite kisses made her feel. Her body was reacting in ways that left her yearning for so much more. It took every ounce of control for her to pull back, but Audrey managed to, knowing this wasn't the time or place. Besides, she needed to know that he was in this for the right reasons.

She met his dark eyes. "Where's this going, Conrad?"

He had been wondering the same thing. *I have to be careful here. Don't want to mess things up by saying the wrong thing.* "Where do you want it to go?"

Her brows knitted. "You answer a question with a question? You'll have to do better than that."

Conrad agreed. What he didn't know was how to answer her. Especially when he couldn't be sure where things would stand between them once he revealed his true identity.

Maybe he needed to have a little faith in her. And himself.

"I think we're both starting to feel something for each other, Audrey," he said evenly.

"You think?" She rolled her eyes wryly.

"Don't you?"

"Of course. But where does that leave us?"

Conrad focused in on her face. "I'd like to continue this and see what happens."

"So are you looking for a long-distance relationship?" Audrey asked bluntly.

He shrugged. "Hadn't really thought about it that way."

"How could you not? Or am I missing something here?"

"You're not." Conrad chewed his lower lip thoughtfully. "I guess I'm just looking for something real that feels right."

Audrey brushed aside a stray hair. Did this feel right? Yes and no. There still seemed to be something missing in the equation, though she was not quite sure what. Or was it simply her imagination? Maybe it would hit her all at once.

"Do you think we can make this work living a few thousand miles apart?" She raised her eyes at him.

Conrad might never have thought such before he reunited with Audrey as a grown woman. Now he believed anything was possible. And he wanted it to be.

"Why not? As long as we're both willing to put forth the effort, I see no reason why we can't succeed."

"You make it sound so simple."

"It doesn't have to be complicated, Audrey."

"I wish I could believe that," she said.

"You can."

Can I?

Audrey had been there, done that and it was hard enough making a relationship work when two people lived in the same city. When that wasn't the case, it made things more difficult even with the best of intentions.

"You don't have a problem becoming involved with the mother of a seven-year-old?" She guessed this would not be a problem in and of itself, but needed to hear him say that.

Conrad did not turn away from her steady gaze. "If you're asking me if I would run away because you have a daughter, the answer is no. I may not know much about being a parent, but I do know something about being a child to loving parents. I also know that Stacy is a great girl and you're a great mother. I respect all that you've gone through in your life and your making something so special of it—including raising a daughter on your own."

Audrey couldn't help but beam, moved by his words. No one had been even close to serious about her in a long time. Was that what Conrad wanted? Did she dare to dream of what they could have together?

Conrad was actually making her believe in things she hadn't in a long, long time: being with someone in a relationship where both were on the same page.

Conrad wished he could read everything in Audrey's mind. He held Audrey again, kissing her and feeling the rippling effect in every nerve.

Audrey kissed him back eagerly and Conrad knew that they had taken that next step, even if he had no idea where it would lead when the dust settled.

"Will you go to church with me?" Audrey asked abruptly, fighting off the tingling sensations Conrad's kiss left on her lips. Since God's house was an important part of her life, she wanted to know that he was at least open-minded in this respect.

The question caught Conrad off guard. He hadn't been to church in a long time, but had never forgotten the place of worship and community he had known before his father's death.

Maybe it will do me some good to attend church service, especially with someone so angelic.

"I'd be happy to," he told her.

"Thank you."

"Thanks for inviting me."

Audrey gently wiped lipstick from his mouth with her pinkie. *Is this man for real?* It seemed as if he was always willing to step up to the plate. She couldn't help but wonder if there was a less than rock-solid side to him. Something told her that Conrad kept some things bottled up inside him, preferring not to share them with her—yet.

Was she simply grasping at straws?

Audrey gave him a soft smile. "Well, we'd better go see where Stacy and Mars have gone off to."

"Good idea." Conrad was sure they were just playing, but knew it would make Audrey feel better to confirm. He also saw it as a good diversion to give them both time to contemplate where things now stood.

They found Stacy and Mars snuggled on the sofa in the sunroom, watching television and seemingly caught up in their own little world.

Conrad wanted to kick himself for delaying the inevitable. Audrey deserved to know who he was, even if that meant putting their blossoming relationship at risk. The thought that he could potentially lose her was almost more than he could bear.

Chapter 15

The next day, Conrad's cell phone rang. He'd hoped it was Audrey, whom he could never get enough of.

Instead her name didn't show up on the caller ID.

"Is this Ulysses Pearson?"

Conrad reacted to the name. "Yes. Who is this?"

"Ben McCray. My son, Willis, gave me your number."

Conrad perked up, glad to hear from the retired firefighter. "Mr. McCray, how are you?"

"I'm doing just fine. So you're Grant Pearson's boy?"

"Yeah."

"Your daddy and I were good friends back in the old days."

"So I've heard."

"I'd love to be able to get together with you and talk about him."

"I'd like that, too," Conrad said keenly.

"If you want to drop by my house this evening, say around six, I can free up my own schedule. I think Willis said that he didn't know how much longer you'd be in town."

It was something Conrad was uncertain of himself, feeling that it depended to a large extent on how things went with Audrey. What he did know was that having a face-to-face with someone who knew his father was an opportunity he couldn't pass up.

"Six sounds good," he replied.

"I'll see you then."

Conrad got directions and then called Jayne to check in on his business.

Ben McCray lived in a brick ranch-style house on a hill. A single oak tree sat in the middle of a snow-crusted lawn. The home was only a few blocks from where Conrad grew up, bringing back vivid memories.

A tall man who looked to be in his early sixties opened the door. He gave Conrad an easy grin and a firm handshake.

"Good to see you again, Ulysses. Come on in, son."

"Nice to see you, too, Mr. McCray," he said respectfully, stepping inside to the foyer and feeling instant warmth.

Ben McCray scratched his scalp through thinning gray hair.

"If your old man were alive now, he'd be damned proud to see that his boy has grown to be taller than him, I expect."

"Yeah, I wish he could see me, too." Conrad swallowed thickly.

"Why don't we go into the den?"

Conrad watched Ben walk across the laminate floor, following him into what looked to be an addition to the old house. A plasma television was on with a college basketball game. Ben grabbed a remote and turned it off.

"Have a seat," he ordered.

Conrad sat on a well-worn recliner.

"Can I get you something to eat or drink?"

Conrad thought about both, but politely declined. "I'm good," he stated.

Ben sat on the couch and stared. "You look a lot like your mother."

Conrad smiled. "I've always been told that, sir."

"How's Isabelle doing anyway?"

"She's hanging in there. Momma remarried a few years after Dad's death."

Ben seemed unaffected by the news. "You know, I used to keep in touch with your momma right after your daddy died," he reflected. "I wanted to make sure if she needed anything, she got it. But soon after she moved, we lost touch. I haven't heard from her in nearly twenty years."

"I think she just needed a fresh start after everything that happened here," Conrad said in her defense.

"Yeah, I guess she would." Ben rubbed his scruffy chin thoughtfully. "That was a dark period for us all. Not a day goes by that I don't wish things had turned out different for your father and the Beaumonts."

"Did you know them, too?" Conrad wondered how much Audrey actually remembered about her own parents.

"We were acquainted. Terrence Beaumont and I used to be in a bowling league together. Neither of us were very good, even though we pretended to be." Ben chuckled gravelly. "Didn't really spend much time with his wife, Margaret, but she knew my late wife, Vivian. They got together with other local young housewives to play cards, talk about soap operas and whatnot. Those were the days...."

He eyed the older man squarely. "What really happened to my father that day, beyond the obvious?"

Ben McCray's brow creased as he sighed. "Well, it started off as a routine house-fire call, to the extent that any can be called routine. Only, by the time we got there, it had gotten out of control. We tried everything we could to get everyone out alive and save the house. Once your father managed to bring the little girl to safety, the house had become too dangerous to go back in. But Grant, who always did think he was a little bit more capable and courageous than the rest of us, thought otherwise. He went back in against my advice and others who were there."

Ben sucked in a deep breath. "Grant got trapped in the flames, along with the Beaumonts. There was nothing we could do, Ulysses, other than add more casualties and sadness to the community."

Conrad watched as tears welled up in Ben's eyes, as if reliving the moment. *I know the feeling and it hurts like hell.* Even if he wanted to blame what happened on his father's colleagues, the Beaumonts or the house itself, Conrad knew, deep down, that these weren't the cause.

"Your father did a good thing in saving little Audrey Beaumont from a certain death," Ben said. "Even if he made the ultimate sacrifice afterward."

"Yeah, he did," Conrad conceded, seeing Audrey in a whole different light now and eternally grateful that his father had played a hand in sparing her life. Maybe it was all somehow meant to go down this way.

"Grant believed to the very end that God was with him. I'm not strong on religion, but I think that maybe your father knew some things that the rest of us didn't. And maybe he's passed some of that insight on to you."

"Not sure I'm deserving of it if he did."

Conrad regretted that he had fallen off the wagon somewhat where it concerned faith after his father's death. Now he wondered if this animosity that had built up inside him like a virus over the years had done little more than make his own life miserable for all the wrong reasons.

Ben coughed. "You are deserving of every bit of your heritage, Ulysses. Maybe not everything in your life has been as smooth as you would have liked, but that's not your fault any more than your father's. None of us are perfect and life ain't easy. We do the best we can and try to learn from our mistakes."

"I get that." Conrad was learning a bit more from his mistakes each day he was in Festive Cove. It was as though everything truly did happen for a reason.

I don't want to make a mistake with Audrey. But how do I rectify previous mistakes without it costing me in trying to build something special between us?

Conrad favored Ben. He could understand how his father had become friends with the man, who seemed to know the right things to say.

"I'm glad Willis saw you at the firehouse," Ben said.

Conrad lifted his chin. "We seemed to hit it off."

"Are you thinking of moving back to Festive Cove?"

"Never say never." Conrad chuckled. The thought was intriguing, though probably not too realistic.

Could a long-distance relationship with Audrey really work? Was it possible that she might be willing to relocate to South Carolina?

Ben sat back. "Willis mentioned that you met with the Beaumont girl?"

"You mean, Audrey?" Conrad's eyes widened.

Ben nodded. "Right, the artist."

"We've gotten together."

"Guess you two have also hit it off, given the ties that bind?"

"You could say that." Conrad was thoughtful.

"Hope you both come away from this on good terms. It's the way it should be."

"I agree." *More than you could possibly realize.*

Ben leaned forward. "Maybe you came back home for a reason, son, one that you're still trying to figure out. That could include leaving South Carolina behind and seeing if you wouldn't be better off where you began your life. I kinda think Grant would be pleased with that, though your mother might have something to say about it."

"She probably would," Conrad voiced with a laugh. But he was his own man and had to do what was best for him. Could be Festive Cove was his destiny after all. If things worked out with Audrey, how could he not seriously consider such a move?

What if his future was calling out to him through this stunning woman and her cute-as-a-button daughter?

With a little help by way of his father from beyond the grave.

Chapter 16

"Can I take just a little peek?" begged Regina. She was standing before the portrait of Conrad that was covered by a cloth.

Audrey, feeling as if she had to uphold her policy of secrecy till the work was done, did not relent. She nudged her friend back a bit and said, "Not until it's completed, girlfriend! Sorry."

Regina batted her lashes outrageously. "And just when will that be...?"

"Hopefully within the next few days."

Audrey felt that was entirely plausible with one more sitting by Conrad and plenty of careful attention to detail. She didn't even want to think about what life would be like for her when he went back to Charleston just as things seemed to be headed in the right direction for them. She would simply have to deal with it one agonizing day at a time.

Regina gazed at the painting as though trying to see through the cloth. "Well, you can't blame a girl for trying, can you? Especially since it seems to be the only way I'll get to have a look at this man who's obviously got you all hot and bothered."

"Actually, there is another way," Audrey told her.

"Let me guess…he's taking out a full-page ad in the paper, photograph and all, declaring his undying love for you?"

Audrey laughed. "Not quite that dramatic, I'm afraid. I've invited Conrad to church on Sunday."

"Oh…?" Regina's eyes grew. "And he accepted your invitation?"

"Sure did. He's coming here and we're riding together," she said enthusiastically.

Regina flashed a big smile. "Well, amen to that! I can hardly wait to meet him."

"I'm sure you'll approve," Audrey teased.

"We'll see. I have to look after my best gal pal."

Audrey embraced her, grateful for Regina's friendship. Good men had been hard to come by. But Conrad was different from the losers she had made the mistake of getting involved with in the past. Not only was he very talented and good-looking, his charm had also worked its magic on her little girl.

Audrey wholeheartedly relished the idea of a serious relationship with him, long-distance or otherwise. Hard as the former may be, the man was definitely worth it.

On Sunday, Conrad felt a bit strange returning to the church he had attended as a boy with his parents. It was like stepping back in time from the perspective of a man in his midthirties. He wondered if this was a good idea. Was it too late to learn to appreciate this spiritual atmosphere?

I don't think so. It's about time I let the Man upstairs back into my life.

Sitting beside Audrey, Conrad couldn't help but think she looked more beautiful than ever. Her hair was in a tight bun, accentuating fine features, and he imagined that she presented the perfect image for another gifted artist to paint a portrait of. Or a certain photographer to capture on film in vivid color.

Conrad turned back to the minister and watched while he introduced the junior choir. They, including Stacy, sang "I'll Be Home for Christmas" beautifully. It moved Conrad as he hadn't been moved in some time listening to holiday music. He slid his fingers between Audrey's, holding her hand. She regarded him with a silent smile and tightened the grip. This told Conrad that they were becoming a real couple. Even if he felt as though there was still a mountain to climb before he could really feel confident about the direction they were headed.

But what better place to have faith in what lay ahead?

Audrey liked the feel of her warm palm pressed against Conrad's. She was proud to be there with him for everyone to see, resplendent as he was in his dark wool suit. She had happily taken a week off from choir to sit by Conrad during the service.

God, please be with Conrad as you are forever with Stacy and me. He has been troubled to some degree ever since I've known him, I believe. Give him the strength to find the inner peace that we all need to feel whole.

Audrey also found herself praying that what she felt for Conrad was genuine and vice versa, and that each would meet the other halfway in overcoming any obstacles that might stand in the way of their forming a loving relationship.

They seemed to be on the right track.

After the service, Audrey introduced Conrad to Regina and her husband, Howard.

"I've been hearing good things about you, Conrad," Regina said, face upturned.

Conrad grinned. "Thank goodness, considering the alternative."

She chuckled. "With a sense of humor, too. Howard, I hope you're taking notes."

Her husband was short with curly brown hair.

"Oh, yeah, baby. I'll try to come up with some good jokes." He winked at Audrey and patted Conrad on the shoulder.

Regina eyed Conrad. "Maybe the four of us can have dinner together sometime before you leave?"

He glanced at Audrey and, believing this worked for her, responded sincerely, "Sounds good to me."

"Great. We'll work on that."

To Audrey this meant that there was no backing out. She was happy to see that Conrad was willing to reach out to her friends. She hoped to return the favor one day.

"I'll call you, girl," she told Regina. "Now, if you'll excuse us, I need to go find my daughter."

That was partly true, Audrey thought. The other part was that she didn't want to make Conrad feel as though he were under the microscope or feel pressured to do anything he didn't want to do.

When they were alone, Conrad said lightheartedly, "Looks like I've won your friends over."

Audrey smiled. "Seems that way. Now, just don't blow it and we'll be fine."

They both laughed.

"I'll try my best not to."

Audrey felt happy that Conrad had come to church with her and was reacquainting himself with the good Lord's teachings, giving her another reason for believing he was someone she wanted in her life.

They located Stacy, who was in the basement

playing with the other children in the choir. Audrey watched as Conrad gave her a hug and told her how much he enjoyed the singing. Stacy ate it up, clearly savoring his admiration, almost like one might a father's attention.

Audrey wondered if she needed to be concerned. Or should she be encouraged that Conrad seemed to want to fill that important role?

Chapter 17

Conrad sat in the tavern, a mug of beer in hand. Two days had passed since he'd attended church with Audrey and Stacy, gravitating toward Audrey in ways he never would have envisioned when he arrived in Festive Cove. Instead of seeing her as someone who would always remind him of the pain of losing his father, Conrad now saw her as a source of strength, inspiration and everything good.

He was falling for the lady hard and fast; and the one thing Conrad didn't want was to hurt her. He was concerned that not being straight about their linked past would leave a cloud hanging over their heads. But he was equally worried that telling Audrey the truth at this stage would ruin everything.

"Are you *with* me, Conrad?"

He looked across the table at Willis, who had apparently said something.

"Yeah, I'm with you, man," he muttered over the rim of his mug. Conrad wished he could confide in him, but didn't see that as the answer right now. Willis might think he was crazy, if not gutless. Either might not be too far from the truth.

"I was saying that my dad enjoyed your visit last week."

"It was good for me, too." Conrad sipped beer.

"That right?"

"Yeah. He's wise and straightforward."

Willis nodded. "Sounds like Pops."

"I wish he and Dad had gotten to know one another in their sixties." Conrad grew melancholy.

"I hear you, man. But, hey, who knows, maybe they'll get the chance to reunite on the other side, so to speak."

"Maybe." Conrad tasted more of the drink pensively.

"I'd like to run something by you, Conrad," Willis gave him a serious look.

"Sure, what's on your mind?"

"With just a week left till Christmas, a friend of mine who manages a mall in town is in need of a short-term photographer to take pictures of Santa Claus with the kiddies. I know it's not your normal gig, but naturally, I thought of you. Interested?"

"Maybe. Tell me more."

"From what I understand, it would last till Christmas Eve, for about four hours a day. The regular photographer is out with the flu."

It hadn't exactly been part of Conrad's plan to ply his trade working for someone else. Especially under crowded mall conditions at Christmastime with possibly more than a few bratty kids to give him headaches. But why not? He might really enjoy it— it would be a far cry from his usual work. And what better way to brighten the faces of vivacious children and their parents than with a photo with Santa that all families cherished?

Conrad wondered if Stacy still believed in jolly old St. Nick? And if her mother still believed in the spirit of Santa Claus.

"Yeah, I'm interested."

Willis grinned broadly. "All right then! I'll give the man a call and get you set up."

"I can hardly wait," Conrad said dryly.

"Hey, now, don't underestimate the photographer's role in the Santa Claus scenario, man."

Conrad smiled. "Wouldn't dream of it."

But there were other things he did have dreams of, such as wrapping his arms around a certain effervescent, beautiful artist with everything to offer to the right man.

Conrad wanted that man to be himself.

Making it happen was the stuff future dreams could be made of.

Audrey moved the brush across the canvas in delicate strokes, hoping to add dimension and character to the unfinished painting of Grant Pearson. She was thankful that Isabelle Pearson was kind enough to provide a good photo for her to work with. While Audrey used this as her guide, she also relied on her memories from the past, weak as they were, and pure creativity and imagination in depicting Grant the human being as much as the firefighter.

An hour later Audrey felt as if she had made some real progress, though she was by no means satisfied that she had achieved a finished product. When it was done, she would know deep in her soul.

Right now she had to go feed her child. Conrad was coming over later for another sitting. Audrey loved painting him, as his features were at once sophisticated and smoothly drawn. All in all, it made for interesting brushwork, different from the Grant Pearson portrait, yet equally intriguing.

She found Stacy in her bedroom, sitting on her teddy bear beanbag chair. A Dr. Seuss book was in her hands and Audrey almost hated to disturb her from what seemed to be Stacy's favorite author. Food, however, was equally important to her developmental growth.

"Time to eat now, honey."

Stacy looked up. "What's for lunch?"

"How about I surprise you?" suggested Audrey, deciding on the spur of the moment that they would go out.

Stacy flashed a tentative smile. "Okay."

"Good. I'll meet you at the front door in five minutes."

Audrey chose McDonald's this time around, knowing Stacy loved fast food, which she was only allowed to eat in moderation. Afterward they went shopping, helping each other pick out clothes.

Audrey dreaded having to soon brave the crowds to purchase the remainder of Stacy's Christmas presents. However, remembering the thrill of receiving and opening gifts from Santa and her parents when she was a little girl, she didn't want Stacy to ever miss out on the wonderful Christmas experience.

Conrad held on to Mars, fearing if he let him run free, the dog might wind up buried beneath a mound of snow. He had decided Mars belonged with someone who could better give him the love and attention a dog deserved. Stacy immediately came to mind.

Conrad rang Audrey's doorbell, glad she had approved of him giving the dog to Stacy. In his mind, they seemed like a perfect match.

As did he and Audrey. But both remained to be seen.

The door opened and Audrey stood there. The look on her face, reacting to Mars as if he were from another planet, told Conrad that she was having misgivings about taking in the dog.

"Hi," Conrad said sheepishly.

"Hey." Audrey met his eyes.

"Can we come in…?"

She paused. "You may."

Audrey wondered if it was really such a good idea to take on a dog and all that it entailed.

"So, where's Stacy?" asked Conrad, looking around as though she were hiding.

"She's up in her room."

"Have you changed your mind about the dog?"

Audrey mused—maybe they could still give it a try. "No, I haven't."

Mars barked and, as if on command, Stacy came running down the stairs.

Her eyes lit. "Hi, Conrad. You brought Mars over for a visit?"

"Actually, there's more to it than that." Conrad glanced at Audrey and then smiled at her daughter. "I wanted to give you Mars, Stacy."

"Really?" She put a hand to her mouth with joy.

"Call it an early Christmas present. Your mom already said it's all right."

Audrey wondered if, by giving away the dog, it meant Conrad was about to leave Festive Cove. And with it, any real chance to see what could develop between them.

"Here's the deal," she told Stacy. "You can keep him but only on a trial basis. And it'll be up to you to make sure Mars behaves and stays away from my studio."

"He will behave, Mommy," Stacy declared. She took the dog from Conrad. Mars licked her face while she hugged him. The two quickly ran toward the stairwell and up to her room.

"Thank you," Conrad whispered.

Audrey's lashes fluttered. "Anything on your mind?"

"Just this…" He bent down and tenderly kissed her mouth, relishing her sweet taste.

Audrey touched her lips which still tingled.

"Any complaints?" Conrad asked, a gentle smile on his face.

"None at all," she said dreamily. *Other than wishing we lived in the same city.*

Conrad beamed and kissed her again. This time he took Audrey in his arms and waited for her mouth to open before drawing her full lips into his while his tongue explored hers.

Audrey returned the favor, feeling light on her feet, and leaned heavily into the man whose potent kiss blew her away. By the time they separated she was breathless and longing for much more intimacy between them.

But that would have to wait. Right now she had a portrait to wrap up.

"Well, are you ready to sit for me?" Audrey was eager to capture his romantic expressions on canvas.

Conrad managed to tone down his libido, hard as that was with Audrey enticing him every moment.

"Ready as I'll ever be to sit still, when I'd much rather continue kissing you."

"Charm will get you everywhere, Conrad," she cooed. "Though not in this case, I'm afraid. The artist in me, who always strives for perfection, must try to keep my eye on the subject in you."

"Oh…" He gazed at her.

"Yes. I want to make sure this portrait is one worthy to give your mother."

Conrad smiled, admiring her work ethic to go along with her uncanny ability to turn him on with just a glance, smile or body movement.

"I have no doubt it will be something she will forever cherish," he said. "With your amazing talent and my mother overjoyed to have a painting of her only child to brag to friends about, it'll be a win-win for everyone."

But what about beyond the portrait?

Conrad wanted his mother to get to know Audrey beyond an exchange of Christmas cards each year. He had a feeling she would be pleased to know that he and Audrey had become romantically involved.

Conrad just hoped that it wouldn't all blow up in his face once Audrey learned that he had not been entirely forthcoming about his identity and purpose for coming to Festive Cove.

Chapter 18

Audrey got caught up in painting her subject, sure this would be one of her finest paintings yet.

Pausing for a moment, her mind wandered to Conrad's implication that his time in town was coming to an end. Parting with Mars was a good clue. What about them? They hadn't really talked about his actual leaving or when he would return. Were she and Stacy invited to visit him? Or was it to be a one-way long-distance romance?

Conrad truly admired the concentration Audrey put into her work, apparently managing to shut off everything else like water from a faucet. He could relate very well. Which was another reason why they had the makings of a great couple, long-distance or not.

"So you must be pretty excited about your show coming up shortly?" he tossed out.

"Not so much excited as nervous anticipation," Audrey said with a chuckle.

"I know what you mean. I've had a couple of shows of my photographs. Great exposure, but it can be nerve-racking wondering what the critics will say, if anyone will show up and so forth."

"Exactly." She changed brushes.

"In any event, I have a feeling that your show will be a highlight of the holiday season in Festive Cove and I wouldn't miss it for anything."

"Thanks for your support, Conrad."

"You're welcome, but I'd say you've earned all the adulation you receive from me or anyone else."

Audrey smiled, happy that Zack had sent him an invitation before she could. Conrad was definitely great for her ego.

"Maybe someday I'll get to go to one of your shows." She hoped he didn't misread that into thinking it was contingent on how their relationship went.

"Nothing would make me happier," Conrad said, resisting the urge to smile with his teeth for fear of interfering with the portrait.

Other than cultivating what we have into a full-blown relationship with endless possibilities.

He noted that the painting of his father was now

covered. Had she done more work on it? Should he inquire about it, risking suspicion on Audrey's part?

"Can you turn your face just slightly that way?" Audrey directed him, as if to get his focus off the painting of Grant Pearson.

Conrad did as he was told, just as others had followed his commands many times in front of the camera. He preferred the latter, but was more than content with the former, considering the beautiful lady giving the orders.

He was still curious about that other painting.

"I couldn't help but notice the covered canvas over there," he said equably. "Is that the one you're working on of the firefighter?"

Audrey nodded nonchalantly. "Yes, it is."

"Gained some *extra* insight or inspiration in adding to the subject?"

She met his gaze. "Something like that."

Conrad paused and then went out on a limb. "I'd love to see it when you're done." He hoped she would take it in the spirit of an art lover and admirer of her work, rather than prying.

"Not sure when that will be," Audrey told him evasively. She was surprised that he seemed to be so interested in the painting. Or was it merely Conrad's way of showing his interest in her by showing an appreciation for the artistic talents she possessed, including in the form of Grant's painting?

Audrey decided to give in a little, as she felt comfortable enough with Conrad to share her vision of the man who saved her life.

"I'll tell you what, before you leave Festive Cove, I'll let you have a peek at the painting of Grant Pearson, as is."

A smile tugged at Conrad's lips, knowing he had gotten Audrey to bend her rules and agree to show him what was obviously a very personal painting to her.

As it was for him.

"It's a deal," he said.

"So when exactly will you be leaving?" she asked straightforwardly.

Conrad sensed some uneasiness in the question. She had every right to ask, considering what was happening between them. He didn't want this to become an issue in and of itself, especially when he had yet to come clean about his background. There was still enough time to talk about the issues of trying to make a long-distance relationship work.

"Probably sometime between Christmas and New Year's Day," he replied honestly, having left the departure date open when coming to town. He wanted to stay longer but had a business to run in Charleston that couldn't be put on hold indefinitely. "Doesn't mean I won't come back. Those frequent-flier miles really come in handy."

Audrey immediately felt as if she had overreacted, if only in her thought processes. *Glad to hear that you intend to come back. Will we be invited to come see you, as well?*

"Just wondered, since you said you weren't able to keep Mars, for which Stacy is eternally grateful, I'm sure."

Conrad blinked. "Well, I suppose I could have taken him back to Charleston, had push come to shove. But it's not really practical with my busy life, especially when I know he can have a home here and be better served."

Audrey could not argue with his logic. She also knew that logic rarely fit into the equation where it concerned matters of the heart.

"There was another reason for giving up Mars at this time…." Conrad admitted.

Audrey stopped painting his chin to look at him. "Oh?"

"I have a job for one week."

Audrey cocked a brow. "You mean, other than the business that brought you to Festive Cove?" *I probably shouldn't have said that. He's not obliged to tell me what he does with his time when not in my company. So long as it's legal.*

Conrad sensed she was suspicious. He had to keep it as real as possible.

"I often travel throughout the country as part of my photography business, conferring with clients and promoting my studio. In the process, I was recruited to fill in as a Santa Claus photographer at the

Oakridge Mall. I intend to donate my earnings to charity." He hoped that was enough to satisfy her for now.

This made Audrey smile. She felt a bit silly wondering what he was up to in Festive Cove as if he were involved in a covert operation for the CIA or Department of Homeland Security. Apparently that couldn't have been further from the truth. She tried to imagine Conrad around a bunch of wiser-than-their-years kids impatiently waiting their turn with Santa. Somehow Audrey was sure Conrad would be more than up to the task.

"Sounds like fun," she said. "And it's very sweet of you."

"We'll see about that," he said. "Can be kind of a real challenge keeping children still enough to take pictures. Especially if they're not getting the right answers from Santa."

Audrey laughed while focusing on Conrad's painted nose, which had just the right depth and texture. "Isn't that the job of a good photographer?"

He grinned. "Indeed."

"Well, now you're getting good practice as a subject that you can apply to your own work."

"Cute." Conrad chuckled. He was only too happy to be her subject, and not only on canvas. If she wanted to take the lead in bed that would work, too. The idea was enticing to him.

He thought briefly as to whether this was the right

time to tell Audrey everything. Maybe her reaction wouldn't be as harsh as he feared. After all, there was never any malicious intent on his part.

That notwithstanding, Conrad felt that were he to spill his guts right now about being Grant Pearson's long-lost son returned home incognito, Audrey just might toss him out on his rear in the snow. And jeopardize the completion of the painting.

Not to mention their burgeoning romance.

I can't allow that to happen. I like her too much to risk losing her now.

"So how were you roped into this choice assignment?" Audrey flashed him an amused look.

"The regular photographer was a bit under the weather and they were in a jam."

"That's nice of you."

"At least it should keep me on my toes." Feeling a bit warm inside, Conrad shifted his body slightly and hoped the artist would not object. "Does Stacy still believe in Santa Claus?" he asked, keeping his voice down.

"Yes." Audrey had not wanted to deprive her daughter of the magic of Santa Claus and his wonderful effect on children for as long as possible. Especially when she herself had been forced to grow up far too soon and lost out on an important part of youth.

"Then why not bring Stacy to the mall to see St. Nick and be photographed by yours truly?" Conrad favored Audrey. "Assuming she hasn't already given her wish list to the chubby man with the white beard and red outfit?"

"Stacy hasn't been to see Santa yet," Audrey uttered, feeling ashamed that she had waited so long to take her to see him. Now it seemed like a blessing in disguise. "Been meaning to, but with work, chores and—"

"In other words, procrastination." Conrad cracked a smile. "Something we're all guilty of every now and then."

"You've got me." She faced him, wrinkling her nose. "Guess it's never too late."

"Never! In this case, it all works out for the best. Stacy can do her thing with St. Nick and I can earn my keep with some great photos of her and the jolly man."

"You're on," Audrey agreed. She was excited at the prospect of taking Stacy to see Santa Claus with Conrad there for encouragement. He would be able to bring out her beautiful smile for the photo.

He inhaled. "I'm sure you already have it covered as far as what Stacy expects from Santa this year?"

A father figure for one, but I'd best keep that to myself at the moment. Otherwise I'm liable to scare Conrad back to Charleston prematurely.

"From A to Z." Audrey laughed. "Or maybe I should have said, one to a hundred."

"Sounds like her wish list is a mile long."

"At least. These days kids not only want but expect everything!"

"Yeah, I'm sure." Conrad fondly remembered the days in which he expected the world for Christmas.

Audrey regarded her handsome subject. Conrad seemed to be deep in thought as if he had suddenly been transported to a faraway land. It was the side of him that he kept to himself like a closely guarded secret. Though piqued, she resisted trying to learn more than Conrad wished to share. If they were to get involved on a serious basis, Audrey imagined that he would come around. Until then, she could wait.

Audrey's mind drifted back to her daughter. "Since Stacy's been a good little girl all year, I think Santa will do his very best to make this a Christmas where her wishes come true."

Or at least those within Audrey's power.

Conrad grinned. "Lucky her. And what about your wishes for Christmas?"

Audrey considered the question. What about them? "Nothing too complicated, really. I just want to make my daughter happy and continue artistry unabated."

"Sounds doable. Anything else?"

I'd also love to end the year by being involved with a wonderful man open to a long-term romance. It's not like I'm asking for the impossible, am I?

Something told Audrey that the man she was painting would play a big part in what could turn out to be another Christmas to remember. Only, it would be full of good memories this time.

She met Conrad's stare. "Let's just say I'm open to whatever comes my way."

His mouth lifted at the corners. "Good answer. I feel the same."

Conrad felt a slight elevation of his heart rate. It had been a long time since he'd viewed the holiday in positive terms. He hoped the bitter would be overcome by the sweet this year. Audrey and Stacy had a lot to do with that optimism. They made him believe that you were never too old for Christmas to bring good tidings.

Including a gorgeous woman who came into his life when he least expected it.

Audrey ran the brush delicately across Conrad's eyebrows while the jet-black eyes below favored her keenly, as though alive. A chill ran up and down her spine and Audrey realized that it was because the man she was painting continued to affect her in ways that brought joy to her heart. And a yearning for whatever the future might bring for them.

Chapter 19

The line of children waiting their turn to sit on Santa's lap seemed to stretch for miles. Conrad stood his ground and patiently snapped picture after picture, happy to lend his talents to provide both parents and children with memories to treasure. Indeed he had his own recollections of a time when believing in Santa and sharing his wish list meant everything. Just as Conrad had once believed that his parents would live forever.

He understood now that childhood beliefs were often at odds with adult realities. However, while Santa Claus would always represent the spirit of everything good for children, adults could also benefit from believing in something greater than themselves and whatever true blessings came their way.

Conrad was coming to terms with the fact that his father was in heaven and far away from the hell that had ended his life way too soon. Just as it had ended the lives of Audrey's parents.

Now was the time to put the darkness of a Christmas past behind him and focus on the light that today's Christmas brought Conrad's way. Audrey and her daughter came to mind.

He smiled when it was Stacy's turn to pour on the charm and get Santa Claus to listen to what she had to say. Being a bright and articulate little girl, Conrad had no doubt that she would succeed. Particularly with her mother within listening distance to make sure that Stacy's wishes had at least a fighting chance of coming true.

Santa Claus hoisted Stacy on his lap and Conrad wasted no time snapping a few pictures. "How about showing some teeth in that smile, Stacy?"

She wasn't shy in obliging his request. He made the most of the moment, amused watching the pair pose perfectly.

Without warning, Conrad turned the camera to Audrey. She tried to wave him off but he was determined to get in a few photos of the beautiful woman who was stealing his heart and giving him a reason to think about someone other than himself. Audrey looked more stunning every time he saw her.

I could take pictures of her all day and night. Of course, she might have something to say about that.

He limited it to two more shots and turned back to Stacy and took a close-up of her face. She gave St. Nick a straight look and made sure she said everything her young mind had conjured up.

Conrad stepped off to the side and couldn't help but listen in on what he expected to be the usual wants from a seven-year-old girl in the twenty-first century.

"...Santa, I want a Barbie doll with her dog, Tanner, and an Easy-Bake oven, and a pretty-princess pony set, and a pink ballet costume, and..."

"And what else?" Santa asked, showing a remarkable patience that probably came with the territory.

Stacy hesitated before saying unevenly, "And I'd like to have a daddy to talk to my friends about at school, go with me and Mommy to church and just have lots of fun with. He doesn't have to come before this year is out, but soon..."

Santa was clearly stumped by that one. He looked to Conrad, as if for answers.

Conrad was speechless, wishing there was something he could say to make Stacy feel her request was plausible. He met Audrey's eyes and was sure that she'd overheard and probably wishing he hadn't. Conrad's heart went out to Stacy, as it was a wish he'd also had for many years before realizing that no one could ever take his father's place. Perhaps the same would prove to be true for Stacy, though she never knew her real father.

It occurred to Conrad that the girl may have been wishing that he could somehow fill those enormous shoes her birth father had left behind. He was both unnerved and flattered by the notion all at once.

A substitute would always be a substitute for the real deal. Wouldn't it?

Did he have what it took to be a father to Stacy or any other child? Was he strong enough to put aside his own bitterness about growing up without a father to turn into the man his own father was?

On the way home, Audrey could only imagine what Conrad was thinking, as neither had talked about the touchy subject in the few minutes after the picture-taking. Her daughter had essentially asked Conrad to be her new daddy and sooner rather than later. And before romance had really blossomed between Audrey and Conrad. Would this frighten him off as it would many men who seemed to run away from any kind of responsibility as if it were a predator?

The last thing Audrey wanted was for Conrad to feel pressured into being a father figure or a husband. It wasn't about that. She was perfectly happy with her life as a single mother and very busy artist. Jumping the gun would be a big mistake for both of them.

I love my daughter dearly. And I'll try to get ninety-five percent of what she wants for Christmas. But that last five percent may be something that only God can make happen.

Audrey wasn't about to read God's mind. Or place unreasonable demands on Him. No, she would just keep an open mind and let things between her and Conrad play out as they were meant to.

And hope that at the end of the day Stacy understood that even Santa had his limits.

Much as Audrey had hers.

Later that evening, Audrey went to her studio and worked on Conrad's painting, as he was fresh on her mind. It was coming along nicely now and in good form. She loved the strong character in his face, the passion in his eyes and the way he seemed to be able to bring out the best in her as an artist.

Inspired, Audrey moved from the painting of Conrad to that of Grant Pearson. They were completely different, she thought, yet similar in the detail and intensity. She loved the process of bringing her subjects to life on canvas and the reward of seeing her completed work.

"Is the fireman still your guardian angel?"

Audrey turned around and saw Stacy holding Mars. Her daughter seemed fixed on Grant's image.

"Didn't hear you come in, honey," she said, though that wasn't too surprising, given her deep focus on the painting. "Yes, he'll always be my guardian angel. Just like you'll *always* be my little angel, Stacy."

She grinned. "Even when I grow up?"

"Especially then. Angels may grow up, but they never leave you."

Mars barked and Stacy asked curiously, "Can dogs be angels, too?"

Audrey smiled. "Well, I suppose they can if you really want them to be. They can certainly be around for a long time as a companion to someone who really cares about them."

"Like me?" Stacy's eyes lit up.

"Just like you, sweetheart." Audrey touched Stacy's nose. "I'll be out of here in just a little while and we can watch a video before you and Mars are off to bed."

The idea clearly agreed with Stacy. "Okay, and I'll pick one!"

"It's a deal."

After she was alone again, Audrey returned to work on the man who saved her life. She ran the brush across the canvas in even strokes and found herself thinking about Grant Pearson's family. Up to now her contact with his widow, Isabelle, had been limited to once a year. Maybe Audrey would give her a call sometime and attempt to build on their relationship.

Audrey was still mildly curious about Grant's son,

Ulysses. All she knew was that he was divorced and
living in Charleston. She wondered why he never responded when she had reached out to him when his
mother had encouraged her to do so.

*The man's probably balding and still carrying
that baby fat while on his third marriage with seven
kids.*

Audrey prayed that his life had been a relatively
good one and that Ulysses was able to remember the
best times when his father was still alive.

For some reason, Audrey found herself thinking
the same thing about Conrad. He hadn't spoken
much about his father, but she could see the pain in
his eyes when he had. Losing a parent was something
one never got over, but in time learned to deal with
to one degree or another.

It was Audrey's hope that someday she and
Conrad would be able to discuss in greater depth
thoughts on death, childhood, parenthood and how
each related to it in their lives.

Until then, she was content to be a part of
Conrad's life and grateful that he had opened his
heart to her and Stacy.

Conrad moved up the walkway of the colonial
revival with a ranch-style design and side porch. It
was the home of his new friend, Willis, and his
family. They were having a pre-holiday meal and had
invited him to join. Though Conrad preferred to be

with Audrey, she was busy painting and didn't need the distraction.

If he played his cards right, they would be giving each other undivided attention soon enough.

Before Conrad could ring the bell, Willis opened the door.

"Glad you could make it," he said, a wide grin on his lips.

"Hard to pass up a dinner invitation and the chance to meet your family." Conrad shook his hand.

"I thought you might bring along a date, man."

"You mean, Audrey?"

"Yeah, unless there's someone else you've got your eye on."

"Only her," Conrad freely admitted, glad that she and Willis didn't travel in the same circles. *Otherwise I'd have some major explaining to do.* "She was tied up."

"Too bad. Maybe next time."

"Maybe." Conrad wasn't sure when that would be, as his days in Festive Cove were numbered. Though Audrey could change that if things worked out for them as he hoped.

Once inside, Conrad was introduced to Willis's wife, Julia. She was petite with brown hair in a flat twist.

"Nice to finally meet you," she said.

"Same here."

"Welcome to our home."

Conrad smiled. "Thanks for inviting me."

"Hope you're hungry," Willis said. "We don't believe in throwing food away."

Conrad chuckled. "You won't have to worry about that."

"Good, though our brood pretty much assures that will never happen."

As if on cue, their three children and two rottweilers came in, gathering around him enthusiastically.

By the time he left, Conrad was envious of this happy family. He wanted to experience such in his life, having wasted too much time on self-pity and blame.

Am I to forever sacrifice who I am and can be by an event that has come and gone? Haven't I suffered enough without further turning my back on the type of life I've longed for?

Conrad rejected the notion that his hands were tied in moving forward. Especially when these days all he could think of was family and stability, with Audrey and Stacy filling the lonely spaces of his existence.

Chapter 20

With just days till Christmas, Audrey made a final push from store to store trying her best to get what remained of Stacy's wish list for Santa.

Of course, her request for a real daddy will take some extra work.

Realistically, Audrey imagined it could be years down the line before that wish could come true for both of them, if ever.

Good men didn't grow on trees. And they certainly didn't fit in red stockings by the fireplace.

Audrey had to admit that Conrad was the type of man who could fit the bill as a husband and father. But there was no reason to jump the gun yet, at least until she knew exactly where he stood on their present and their future.

After spending much of the day shopping, Audrey came home with bags and boxes, grateful that Stacy and Mars were at Regina's while she played Santa Claus. She had also purchased a gift for Conrad that seemed apropos and hoped he would like it.

She carefully wrapped some gifts, putting them under the tree, and hid others to bring out on Christmas Eve at about the time Santa was due to arrive.

At this point Audrey couldn't wait till the big day.

But first she had a date with Conrad. It was time at last to unveil his portrait.

Conrad stood at his father's grave, a solitary figure but far from alone. He recalled Audrey standing in that very spot the first time he saw her in twenty-five years. He hadn't wanted to intrude upon her space or have her infringe on his. Now Conrad wished he had done things differently that day. Had he introduced himself as Ulysses Pearson from the start, it wouldn't be so damned difficult to do so now.

If he had, would things have progressed between them to the same degree? Would Audrey have opened up to him as much had she known he was the psychologically damaged son of the man who saved her life many years ago?

Maybe this was the way it was supposed to be.

He wanted to believe that all things happened for

a reason. In this case, to give two people a second chance at happiness. He was more than ready to take that chance. He just wondered if Audrey would be willing to take the chance, as well.

Conrad walked away from the cemetery and didn't look back, deciding he had done enough of that in his life. There was a path ahead of him that he was determined to navigate, no matter the bumps and rough edges he was sure to encounter along the way.

He stopped at a florist and purchased a long-stemmed red rose. Seemed like the perfect thing to present to a perfect lady.

"This is for you," Conrad said, proffering the rose.

Audrey's face glowed as she put the flower to her nose and enjoyed its fragrance. It was the first time anyone had given her a rose—other than the one she received from one of her clients who'd loved the portrait she'd done. But this was entirely different and it meant so much more to Audrey coming from Conrad.

"It's lovely," she gushed.

"So are you." Conrad looked deeply into her eyes.

"Oh…you're so sweet." After walking into the living room, she gave him a soft kiss, forcing herself to release his lips. "I'll just go put this in water to keep it fresh as long as possible."

"There's more where this one came from, Audrey."

"True. But there can only be one first, Conrad."

A grin dimpled his cheeks. "You always know the right things to say."

She smiled. "I'm not so sure about that. I'll take the compliment nonetheless."

"So where are Stacy and Mars?" Conrad had expected them to practically spring out of the woodwork when he arrived.

"They're at Regina's. I don't expect her to bring them home for another couple of hours."

A glint appeared in his eyes. "I like the sound of that."

Audrey colored. "I thought you would. First thing's first." She paused. "It's time to see yourself on canvas."

Conrad smoothed an eyebrow, eager for the unveiling. "Can't wait."

"You won't have to much longer. Be right back." Her eyes met his. "Stay right here. And no peeking, either."

He laughed. "Wouldn't dream of it." *Anything worthwhile is worth waiting for. Including you.*

Audrey was nervous, as she always was whenever she was about to show work she had been commissioned to do. What if Conrad found it lacking? Maybe her vision would fall well short of his own? Could the strength of the painting affect that of their relationship or any potential future?

Conrad could tell that Audrey was on edge, as if this would be a defining moment for them both. Admittedly he was a bit tense, too. It was the first time anyone had ever put him on canvas and he was intrigued to see how he measured up to other oil portraits he'd seen. Like the one of his father currently on display at the fire station.

I doubt a painting of me could ever compete with what many consider a masterpiece.

"Are you ready?" Audrey asked, butterflies in her stomach.

"Ready as I'll ever be." Conrad gave her a genuine smile. "Let's do it."

"Okay." There was no turning back now and Audrey trusted her talents to win out, as was usually the case. After sucking in a deep breath, she lifted the cover and the portrait was revealed.

Conrad stared at himself, frozen with astonishment. The larger-than-life image shocked him for its likeness, clarity and depth. The notion that Audrey had been able to put forth the true essence of who he was in this vibrant portrait amazed him. He wasn't sure if his photographs of people had nearly the same impact.

"Well, what do you think?" Audrey asked, heart pounding. "Don't keep me in suspense, Conrad. And, please, be perfectly honest."

"I wouldn't be anything but honest," he promised, and studied himself again before facing her. "I absolutely love it! You've made me look much better than I ever could in real life."

Audrey released the breath she had been holding

on to like a sack of heavy air. She loved it, too, feeling she had captured every magnificent feature in his handsome face. Though she doubted anything could look better than the real man.

"I'm glad you like it," she said, playing down her own satisfaction. "I always aim to please my clients."

"Well, you've certainly done that and more!" Conrad continued to be awed by the portrait. It was the last thing he'd had in mind when he came to Festive Cove. Now he couldn't imagine not having had the painting done.

Audrey batted her lashes. "Do you think it will meet with your mother's approval?"

"No doubt about it! She'll think this painting is the greatest thing since...well, probably since the time I sent her and my stepfather on a cruise to the Hawaiian Islands five years ago. But this is even better since Momma will be able to look at and appreciate the painting anytime she wants."

"Better her than you," quipped Audrey. "Wouldn't want you to get too big of a head."

Conrad laughed and touched his temples. "Probably couldn't get much bigger than it already is."

She loved his sense of humor and felt relieved that he was happy with her work.

"Thank you for doing the portrait on such short notice." Conrad felt a little guilty in initially using it as a pretext for getting to know her better and learning more about his father's last day of life.

Audrey's cheeks colored. "I'm glad I did it. You were a great subject."

He put his arms around Audrey's small waist and pulled her closer. Her body was soft and sexy. They seemed perfect together.

"I'm all about keeping one's skills sharp."

"Oh…" Audrey's pulse quickened.

"Very much so."

"Why don't you show me something you think you're skilled at?"

"With *pleasure*."

Conrad angled his lips down to Audrey's mouth. Like the previous times, he thoroughly enjoyed kissing her, using his tongue to probe the tastiness she dispensed. It reminded him of what he had been missing for so long and what he never wanted to be without again.

Audrey savored the power of Conrad's lips, matching her own in feeling one another out and raising the temperature considerably. She wrapped her arms around Conrad as if he were her captive, though Audrey was also every bit his prisoner.

Conrad's erection threatened to tear through his trousers, aching to be inside her. They had waited long enough to take their relationship to the next level. He hoped Audrey agreed and gave herself to him.

"I want to make love to you, Audrey," he whispered against her mouth.

"Me, too," she murmured, having imagined them

being together many times. Now the time seemed right. "Do you have protection?"

"Yes." Conrad made it his business to be responsible, not wanting to risk pregnancy till such time, if ever, that it was something they both wanted.

Audrey smiled, glad that little issue was quickly resolved, leaving them to focus on each other. "Then I'm all yours, Conrad...."

"Music to my ears." He kissed her again, feeling the rise of her nipples tickling his chest.

"Let's go upstairs...." Her voice was husky.

"Lead the way...." Conrad's pulse raced with anticipation of what was to come.

Audrey took his hand and led him from the studio, eager to make love to the man who had her totally hooked.

In her bedroom, Audrey felt slight jitters as anyone would when having sex with someone for the first time. She wanted to please Conrad and not appear inept. Maybe he felt the same way, even if he was probably more experienced.

In plunging ahead in this relationship, Audrey wanted to convey in actions what Conrad was starting to mean to her as a woman. Through intimacy she hoped they would bond in a way that left them both starving for more.

Conrad took one sweeping glance around the room, impressed with its size and interior decoration.

But none of it held a candle to the lady of the house. He focused on Audrey, mesmerized by her sheer beauty and femininity. They stood at the foot of the bed while he gently caressed her face. He could feel Audrey trembling. Or was he the one shaking?

"You're driving me crazy, baby." His voice deepened lasciviously. "Positively insane with desire."

"That works both ways," Audrey cooed, delighted to know she had this effect.

Conrad cupped Audrey's cheeks for a deep, mouth-watering kiss before starting to remove her clothes. He admired her smooth and taut body every step of the way, beginning with her high breasts that were small but full. The nipples protruded and were a turn-on all on their own. He could only imagine how much the rest would tantalize.

Taking this cue, Audrey began unbuttoning Conrad's shirt, exposing his muscular chest, then undid his pants with much keenness as to what she would find within. She was barely cognizant of her own nakedness to his hungry eyes, so strong was her need for this man.

Conrad effortlessly lifted her into his arms and brought her to the bed, gently laying her down. Audrey watched as he removed a condom and slipped it onto his massive manhood, making her slightly dizzy with yearning at the prospect of him being inside her momentarily.

"Let me enjoy you before we enjoy each other,"

Conrad said, ignoring the demand of his erection, aching for her.

"Enjoy as much as you want," Audrey said, hiding the fact that she wasn't used to much more than intercourse in bed. Apparently that was about to change.

Conrad kissed Audrey's neckline, moving down between her breasts. He licked there before applying hot kisses and caresses to both nipples, feeling them swell beneath the onslaught of his tongue. At same time, he put a hand between her legs, where she was hot and moist.

"Oh…Conrad…" she moaned. "That feels so good."

It was all Audrey could do not to climax on the spot. She bit down on her lower lip, willing herself to hold back.

Conrad had other notions. "You deserve everything I'm giving you and so much more," he insisted, continuing to pepper kisses down her body, leaving goose bumps in his wake.

When he put his face between her legs, Conrad had no doubt that he was pleasing himself at least as much as Audrey. He kissed her most precious spot, loving every moment as she reacted. He held on to her thighs firmly and continued to feast in warming her up for their union.

Audrey lost control as the waves of pleasure washed over her. Her body jerked and her breath quickened at the moment of impact. Now she needed Conrad inside her more than ever.

She clutched his shoulders and commanded, "Take me—now!"

"I will," Conrad responded, lifting up, his own libido in overdrive.

He lowered himself inside her splayed legs and thrust deep into her body, enjoying the tightness within. Conrad's eyes glazed at the beautiful and sexy person beneath him who felt every bit as good as he'd envisioned.

"Kiss me," Audrey pleaded, wanting to come again with their mouths and bodies locked in perpetual motion.

Conrad obeyed, his mouth descending upon hers, kissing with renewed urgency as each attacked the other, their tongues joining in the frenetic passion. He felt the surge begin to rise within him and held his breath as a thunderous orgasm erupted.

Audrey held Conrad's quivering body tightly, waiting till the last possible moment before she joined him in the pure ecstasy of sexual gratification.

They soared together like eagles, reaching new heights in their union before coming back down to earth, each spent and satiated.

Afterward Audrey melted in Conrad's comforting

arms, wanting nothing more than to enjoy his embrace, if only for a while.

"You were *amazing*." Conrad's warm breath fell onto her brow.

"So were you." She looked up. "Like you had any doubt."

He chuckled. "Maybe not, but I have to stay away from that big head you alluded to earlier."

Audrey laughed naughtily. "Hmm…no comment."

Conrad slid a hand down her leg till he reached a wet place. "None whatsoever."

She made a humming sound as he stimulated her. "You're wicked."

"And you aren't?" He curled her pubic hairs around his finger, feeling himself aroused again. "Care to go a second round?"

Audrey hummed again, fighting the growing needs this man was instilling within her with even the slightest touch. Not to mention when he went further than that.

"I'd really love to. But I think Stacy and Mars will be back anytime now. How about we freeze that thought till the next golden opportunity presents itself?"

Conrad was not about to argue against it. Audrey was too special to want to screw things up. Certainly not by demanding more of her time than she had to spare. If Conrad was going to become a regular part

of Audrey's life, he would have to get used to them
dividing their time between work, Stacy, themselves
and even Mars.

He kissed her shoulder. "It's a deal."

Chapter 21

"You'll be just fine," Conrad assured Audrey, accompanying her to the show. *But will I? What if someone from the firehouse recognizes me as Grant Pearson's son before I break the news to Audrey? She would probably hate me or worse.*

On the other hand, he couldn't very well back out of the event with no reasonable excuse. Not after they had consummated their relationship. Audrey needed him there for support and Conrad wanted to be there for her big moment. It was worth the risk of exposure.

"I know." Audrey put on a brave face, comforted by Conrad's words and presence. It was quite natural to have jitters when facing an audience of judges, some who were likely wannabe artists quick to point out any flaws in the works. Overall, though, she expected a largely receptive gathering and wanted to make the most of it.

She glanced at Conrad behind the wheel. As usual, he was a magnificent sight and as handsome as ever in his dark gray suit. Audrey was delighted he was her date and new boyfriend, though they had not defined their relationship as such. *How else would you refer to someone you started sleeping with and had gotten so close to intellectually and spiritually?*

"So how did Zack get so fortunate to exclusively handle your works of art?" Conrad favored Audrey casually. "Seems like there's no shortage of art galleries in Festive Cove."

She smiled. *Do I detect a little jealousy? I suppose there's nothing wrong with that. It shows he must really like me.*

"I've known Zack since college. He was one of my early supporters. So when I 'made it,' Zack was the first one in town to offer to sell my paintings. It's worked out well. He continues to be a strong advocate of my work and a good friend."

"That's nice to know." Conrad gave an awkward half smile.

"There's never been anything between Zack and me if that's what you're wondering," Audrey made clear.

"Didn't think so. Just curious, that's all."

"Yeah, right." She rolled her eyes skeptically. "Right now the only man in my life is you, Conrad."

He took this to heart. *I hope it stays that way even after you know my true identity.*

"And the *only* woman in my life is you," he responded, "along with a pretty little lady named Stacy."

Conrad wanted to kick himself for being territorial. Audrey deserved her successes in life, including having people like Zack stick by her through thick and thin.

Just as I intend to if she will let me.

They stopped at the door of Beauty In Art. Conrad took a final look at Audrey. She was perhaps as beautiful as he'd ever seen her, wearing a lace-trimmed aubergine shirtdress with her hair in an attractive little ponytail.

"How about a kiss for luck?" he asked.

Audrey flashed her teeth, welcoming any chance to kiss him. "*Just* for luck?"

Conrad grinned. "All right, because I love kissing you and now seems as good a time as any."

She wasn't about to disagree, even if it meant getting lipstick on his mouth. "You're right, it is."

Conrad bent down to her tilted face and brought their lips together. The kiss was short but very sweet.

"So let's do this," he said. "Your audience awaits."

Audrey took a breath, mentally preparing herself for what she hoped to be a successful show. "Then let's not keep them waiting...."

* * *

Audrey was greeted by Zack, who wore a black tuxedo. He kissed her on the cheek. "Welcome to your event."

"Wouldn't have missed it for the world," she kidded, taking the flute of champagne he offered her.

"Thank goodness." Zack gave her the once-over. "You're looking lovely as always."

"Thank you." Audrey blushed and eyed Conrad. He seemed to take it all in stride.

Zack turned to Conrad, extending his hand and another champagne flute. "Ah, Conrad. Glad you could make it."

Conrad shook his hand, offering a smile. "Like Audrey, I wouldn't want to be anywhere else this evening."

"Then we're all definitely on the same page." Zack's eyes widened. "As you can see, many others shared your sentiments."

Audrey took in the gathering that had come to see her paintings. The turnout was more than she could have expected and she felt humbled.

"Hey, girlfriend," she heard five minutes later.

Audrey saw Regina and Howard approaching. "Hey, you."

"Wondered if you'd show up to your own shindig," Regina said lightheartedly.

Audrey laughed. "Had to be fashionably late, you know that." In fact, it was just the opposite.

Regina fluttered her lashes at Conrad. "I think you have a pretty good excuse."

"Good to see you again, Regina." Conrad's lips curved upward. "You, too, Howard."

"Likewise," he said, shaking Conrad's hand. "Nice collection you've got here, Audrey."

"Thanks, Howard. Means more to hear my friends say that."

"He's just trying to butter you up to get a painting at a serious discount," quipped Regina.

"Anytime," Audrey said.

"Won't be long before they're selling for a mint online," Howard suggested.

"Probably," Conrad agreed, assuming that wasn't already the case. He couldn't be more proud of Audrey and wanted her to soak this up as he had during shows of his work.

A familiar voice drew Conrad's attention. Approaching them was the Festive Cove fire chief, Hamilton Long, his wife by his side. Conrad momentarily froze.

Damn! I can't let Audrey find out about me this way. I've got to disappear and hope I don't come up in a conversation.

With a weak smile pasted on his lips, Conrad got Audrey's attention. "I think I'll go for another flute of champagne. Catch up with you in a bit."

"I could use another, too," Howard said.

"Go ahead then." Regina frowned. "I'm sure we girls can survive without you."

Audrey chuckled while hoping Conrad hadn't gotten bored already. "See you," she said, and watched as his smile brightened, making her feel that this wasn't the case.

She turned her attention to Hamilton Long.

"That's one hell of a painting," Howard remarked, staring up at one of her seascapes.

"Yeah, she did a fantastic job." Conrad regarded the painting that Audrey had held on to especially for this show. Her talents never failed to amaze him.

Howard sipped his champagne. "Maybe I'll commission Audrey to do a portrait of me and Regina to mark our third anniversary next year."

"Sounds like a good idea. If you need a testimonial, give me a call."

Howard grinned. "I'll make a note of that." He regarded Conrad beneath thick brows. "So when do you plan to make an honest woman out of Audrey, man?"

This made Conrad chuckle uneasily. The idea of marrying Audrey had much appeal, as he was sure she would make a perfect bride. But it was too soon to go there. Not until they cleared up a few things and saw where the dust had settled.

"Your guess is as good as mine," he said honestly. "Right now we're taking things nice and slow, and will see what happens."

"Makes sense. Don't want to rush into anything and have it come back to haunt you later."

"Tell me about it. Been there, done that." Conrad thought of his ex. She was nothing like Audrey. He was confident that had he married Audrey back then they would have long ago gotten past the Christmas Day fire and made a good life for themselves.

But fate had never intended for that to happen. Their time was here and now and they had to make the most of it or lose whatever ground they had gained.

"You've really given this town something to be proud of," Hamilton Long said, half-filled flute in hand.

Audrey colored. The fire chief had been so enthusiastic when he had accepted her offer to donate a portrait of Grant Pearson to the fire department. She was grateful for that, as it had allowed Audrey to make restitution to some degree for the death of a great man.

"The town has given me so much more back," she said.

"I don't know about that."

"You're a great talent, Audrey," Hamilton's wife, Sandra, said. "I'd love to be able to paint. I especially loved the painting you did of Grant Pearson that is up at the firehouse."

"It was something that came straight from the heart. Thank you so much."

Hamilton's cell phone rang. He frowned as he reached for it. "I'd better get that."

"Excuse me," Audrey whispered to his wife. She gave a little wave and then went off to circulate.

Audrey jumped when she felt Conrad come up behind her. She turned to see him smiling tenderly.

"Miss me?" he asked.

"What do you think?" She gave him a teasing look.

"I think you're utterly terrific."

Audrey's eyes shimmered. "Good answer."

"My momma didn't raise no fool," Conrad voiced wittily.

"You're right about that. She raised a wonderful man."

Audrey couldn't help but be as honest with him as he had been with her. Men such as Conrad were definitely hard to find. Meaning Audrey had to do what she could to not let this one get away.

Chapter 22

That Sunday, December 23, Conrad stood behind the long table filled with trays of turkey, ham, cornbread dressing, mashed potatoes, green beans, biscuits and sweet potato pie. He had volunteered to assist in the Christmas week Feed the Needy program, organized by the community and sponsored annually by the Festive Cove Fire Department. It was something Conrad remembered his father doing and he was happy to be able to contribute his own time to this worthy cause.

"You're a natural at this, Conrad," said Willis, passing out scoops of dressing to a lineup of homeless and disadvantaged people.

"Not that hard to put some food on plates." Conrad downplayed the task at hand.

"Yeah, that's true, but you'd be surprised just how many people come up with every excuse in the book as to why they can't pitch in for those less fortunate. Which explains why we were shorthanded on volunteers this year."

"Well, I'm glad I could pitch in." Conrad smiled at the elderly woman before him as he placed a couple of slices of turkey on her plate.

"God bless you," she said in a hoarse voice.

"I believe God has definitely blessed me," he responded thoughtfully, and began counting his blessings. He had been blessed with great health over the years and a talent that had made his life easy by the standards of many. His mother and stepfather were still alive and going strong, which was more than some could say. Conrad had survived a bad marriage without losing the better part of himself in the process.

He had even made peace with his father after carrying around baggage for years like a dead weight.

And, most recently, Conrad had found in Audrey a possible soul mate, someone he could envision spending the rest of his life with if she would have him.

Yes, I'd say the Lord Almighty has certainly blessed me even when I couldn't see it staring me right in the face until now.

"If you really feel so inspired, we have another Feed the Needy program coming up at Easter," Willis half joked. "You can always come back and you'll be welcomed with open arms."

"I'll keep that in mind." Conrad cracked a tiny smile. In fact, he had been giving some serious thought to staying in Festive Cove a lot longer than originally planned. Maybe he could open up a studio here while keeping the other one going in Charleston. He planned to run the idea by Jayne to see if she was up for a promotion.

The thought of being away from Audrey for any great length of time was actually painful for Conrad to think about. She was becoming more and more important to him with each passing day. He wanted to be there for her and Stacy. Of course, how long he remained in Festive Cove would largely depend on how Audrey took the news that he wasn't Conrad but Ulysses Pearson, Grant's only son.

Conrad had made the decision to tell her tonight. He had invited Audrey to a home-cooked meal, where he intended to fess up and throw himself at her mercy. He could only hope that the God-fearing woman in Audrey would be understanding and not turn her back on their relationship.

Failure was not an option in Conrad's mind, though he wasn't sure Audrey would see eye-to-eye on that.

"I think I'm in *love*," Audrey said, sitting in a packed coffee shop with Regina.

The words were both alarming and exhilarating as Audrey thought about what they might mean to her life. Yet she couldn't deny what her heart knew was true.

Regina rolled her eyes. "Why am I not surprised? Who wouldn't be in love with a man who seems to have it all going for him?" She held up her fingers to count. "He's very good-looking, smart, successful, single, sincere, he adores Stacy... Oh, and he's actually available. Most importantly, the man knows a good thing when he sees it in you, girlfriend!"

Audrey blushed over her cup of mocha. "But I'm not sure I'm ready to be in love," she said uneasily. "Being a single mother and a professional artist can take so much out of me. Add love to the mix and I'd really have a balancing act to play."

Regina's brows lowered. "Will you listen to yourself, Audrey? Stop being ridiculous! Love doesn't come when you're ready, it just comes, ready or not. You've had enough deadbeats in your life, starting with you-know-who. You deserve someone like Conrad who will treat you with the respect you're entitled to. And since he has his own successful business, he won't be intimidated by your success."

Audrey tasted her drink and contemplated Regina's words. *I do deserve the best and will be the best woman for the right man. But is Conrad the right man? Yes, he's hot and great in bed to go along with all the other superlatives. So why am I second-guessing what seems to be a near-perfect fit?*

"I'm just a little freaked out by the long-distance thing," she admitted.

"Well, don't be," Regina scoffed. "Last I heard Charleston was not like going to the moon. Or even Kenya, where Howard and I vacationed last year. Besides, maybe Conrad will relocate here...."

"Yeah, maybe."

Audrey pondered the possibility. They hadn't exactly gotten into that kind of discussion. More like they had dodged it as though that might make it somehow disappear. Would Conrad actually consider permanent residence in Festive Cove? Or would he be satisfied with a back-and-forth romance—meaning separate lives?

"There's nothing preventing you from moving to Charleston down the line, Audrey, if that's what it takes to hold on to this great man."

"Nothing other than that I've lived in Festive Cove the better part of my life, have established my studio here, and it's a place where Stacy seems happy. Uprooting her and myself for—"

"The opportunity to spend your life with the right man in, from what I've heard, one of the most exciting cities in the South." Regina shot her a puzzled look. "C'mon, girlfriend, that's pretty much a no-brainer. But then, that's just me."

Audrey bristled. "I'm not even sure Conrad and I are on the same page concerning a long-term relationship." Were they? She had once been willing to go anywhere for a man, only to be stung, left pregnant and all alone. Was Conrad a man who was trustworthy and dependable through thick and thin?

I need to know for sure that he is the real deal and not just smoke and mirrors.

Regina sipped on a café con leche. "Then don't you think it's time you found out before you give away your heart and can't get it back?"

I'm afraid it might already be too late for that.

"Yes, I do." Audrey sat back thoughtfully. "Conrad's cooking me dinner tonight. I'll probably get up the nerve to tell him my concerns and hope I don't make a complete fool out of myself."

"I doubt that. It's pretty clear to me this is anything but a one-sided relationship. If I read those alluring eyes of Conrad's right, that man is absolutely crazy about you."

"You think?" Audrey asked with tilted head.

"I *know,*" stated Regina. "Howard picked up on it, too. But let Conrad speak for himself. I don't want to spoil it."

Audrey's cheeks lifted, warmed at the notion that Regina had hit the nail on the head. Now it was about time that Conrad stepped up to the plate and did the same.

Chapter 23

It had been a while since Conrad had made a real home-cooked meal for anyone. But he challenged himself to do it for Audrey. Not only did he want her to sit back and just enjoy, this was the night he would reveal his true identity and let Audrey know how far back they really went. Conrad wasn't sure how Audrey would take the news or how he might were the situation reversed. What he did know was that there was never any harm intended or deception, per se, in his less-than-full disclosure. He just hoped she could get past it and look at the big picture.

The bottom line was that he had truly grown to care for Audrey and wanted things to work out for them from the bottom of his heart.

Would Audrey feel the same when all was said and done?

Guess I'll just have to wait and see.

Trying to think positive, Conrad focused on preparing pork chops, mushroom gravy, black-eyed peas, mashed sweet potatoes and banana bread. He had also purchased an expensive bottle of chenin blanc. He wanted this dinner to be special for more reasons than one.

Aside from wanting to get something off his chest long overdue, Conrad was also ready to admit what he had never expected to at this time in his life, if ever again. He had fallen in love with Audrey and wanted this to work between them more than anything he could remember. He sensed that her feelings toward him were strong, too. What he didn't know was how much damage might be done to their relationship after he said his piece.

I'd rather look at the glass half full. Maybe if I ply Audrey with enough wine it'll soften the blow.

Conrad found himself doing something he hadn't done in some time. He prayed to God that he hadn't blown it with Audrey.

In his heart and soul, Conrad saw Audrey as the key to putting behind them the pieces of the fractured history they shared. But there were no guarantees. She might look at things from the opposite end of the spectrum. And where would that leave them?

For the time being Conrad could only count the

minutes till Audrey arrived and see which way the pendulum swung.

He sat on that unnerving thought for a moment, before tending to the food.

The snow was coming down in hexagon flakes and Audrey took note of how beautiful they looked at night, covering the landscape like a blanket. She would gladly take a winter wonderland every Christmas if she didn't have to drive in it. She peeked through the rearview mirror and saw Stacy bundled up in the backseat, holding Mars.

"Are you two doing all right back there?"

"Yeah," Stacy said in a lazy voice, petting Mars to much the same effect.

"Good, won't be long now." She was dropping Stacy off at her friend's house for a few hours while Audrey had dinner alone with Conrad. If things went as planned, there would be plenty of time later to include Stacy in outings.

Maybe even someday as a real family.

It made Audrey think of how much she missed her parents and wished with all her heart that they were still around. Why had life been so cruel to deprive her of two of the most important people in shaping her own life? Her adoptive parents had done their best to fill the void, but she always felt something missing.

At least things seemed to be looking up at the

moment as far as the importance of growing relations was concerned. Thanks in large part to Conrad.

Stacy's friend, Abigail Everly, lived in a Spanish-style home, distinguished by its red tile roof, stuccoed exterior and large, front-facing windows. Tonight the entire thing was a mass of synchronized flashing colorful lights, which extended to the maple tree occupying the front lawn.

Audrey admired the light show as she pulled into the driveway behind two other cars, noting several more parked along the curb. Between that and the music coming from the house, it was obvious the Everlys already had company. Audrey briefly considered taking Stacy to Conrad's house, but since Abigail was expecting her, it wouldn't be fair to either girl to deprive them of spending time together.

"Now, remember that Mars is *your* responsibility," Audrey warned her daughter as Stacy carried the dog toward the house. "Don't let him get into something that will only spoil your visit and cause the Everlys to get on my case."

Stacy did not look concerned at all. "I won't," she promised. "Mars knows how to behave like a good doggie. Don't you, Mars?"

The dog barked in response and Stacy smiled as if having proven her point. Audrey was less than convinced, but gave her the benefit of the doubt that they would stay out of trouble.

The ringing of the bell produced an immediate response and friendly greetings.

"Come on in and say hello to everyone, Audrey," Estelle, Abigail's mother, said after Stacy and Mars had run off with Abigail.

Audrey was eager to be on her way, hopefully Conrad was just as anxious to have her there. But she decided it wouldn't be very polite to dump Stacy off on them and just leave. She smiled at the pretty woman with sable crinkled locs.

"Well, okay, just for a few minutes," she told her.

Inside there was instant warmth and the smell of fried chicken, which Audrey tried to ignore as her dinner this night lay elsewhere. The sound of Nat King Cole's "The Christmas Song" blended in with chatter and laughter as she was led through rooms decorated for Christmas to the family room.

"Everyone, say hello to Audrey, Stacy's mother," Estelle voiced enthusiastically.

Audrey recognized Estelle's husband, Luther, along with the Festive Cove firefighter Willis McCray, sitting next to his wife, Julia. Audrey wasn't familiar with the other couple, Oliver and Gail Nolte, who were holding hands and seemingly very much into each other.

"Merry Christmas," she told them, lifting a hand awkwardly to wave.

Audrey imagined poor Conrad slaving over the stove, hoping his meal turned out right. For her part, Audrey was more concerned with what came during and after the meal once she laid her feelings on the line and then waited to hear his.

As though forgetting his manners, Willis stood and approached Audrey. He stuck a long arm out.

"Nice to see you again, Audrey."

"You, too, Willis," she said, shaking his hand. They had met at the firehouse when Audrey donated the portrait of Grant. Willis seemed friendly enough and had actually seemed genuinely interested in her artwork.

He looked at the Noltes and said, "This here is one of the greatest talents we have in Festive Cove. Audrey is an artist extraordinaire."

"Oh, yeah…?" Oliver looked intrigued.

"The man knows what he's talking about," Luther added, as if only to get involved in the conversation. "I've seen her work."

Before Audrey could escape the unwanted attention, Willis went on, "One of Audrey's paintings is on display at the fire station. It's of one of our fallen comrades, Grant Pearson."

Oliver's face sagged. "Sorry to hear about that firefighter."

Gail seconded this. "That's terrible."

"It was a long time ago," Audrey said, though it sometimes seemed like only yesterday.

"Can I get you something to eat or drink, Audrey?" Estelle asked, as though simply to change the gloomy subject.

"No, thank you," she responded. "I'm, uh, having dinner with a friend. On that note, I should probably get going…."

"That's fine. And don't worry about Stacy. Abigail is thrilled to have her and Mars to play with while us grown folks talk."

"I'm glad to hear that." The last thing Audrey wanted was to feel that Stacy was an imposition.

Willis, who had sat back down, seemed amused when he said to Audrey, "That friend wouldn't happen to be Ulysses Pearson, would it?"

Audrey cocked a brow. Ulysses Pearson? Why on earth would he think that? As far as she knew, Ulysses lived in Charleston. Had he moved back to Festive Cove?

"If you're referring to Grant's son—I haven't seen him since he moved away with his mother many years ago. I'm actually dating a man named Conrad."

Willis viewed her, looking nonplussed.

"I think we're talking about the same person," he said. "I don't know what's up with the Conrad name—unless it's his alter ego. We met when Ulysses dropped by the firehouse earlier this month to check out the painting of his dad. From what I understood, the two of you have been spending time together catching up ever since. If I'm mistaken…"

Audrey's knees shook while trying to digest what she'd just heard. *Conrad is Ulysses Pearson?* Grant's *son…?* The boy she knew so long ago.

If it was, why would he tell her that his name was Conrad? Why wouldn't he have told her that his dead father was Grant Pearson? None of it made any sense. Or did it?

Audrey thought back to the first time she saw Conrad at the cemetery. He seemed to be headed to Grant's gravesite, but went to another instead, as if making up his tale along the way.

If Conrad was Grant's son, why did he lie about it? What did he possibly hope to gain by playing with her emotions?

Only my heart, which he'd managed to crush.

Or had that been the plan all along—to somehow get back at her for his father's death—strange as that sounded? Had Isabelle Pearson known about this setup?

Once Audrey left, she drove around in circles as though she had lost her sense of direction. She couldn't imagine that the man she had fallen in love with had turned out to be nothing but a fraud. It was difficult for Audrey to wrap her head around why Conrad would keep his true identity to himself.

Was he honest about anything in their so-called relationship? What the hell were the lies about?

Part of Audrey wanted nothing more to do with Ulysses Pearson, but she found herself driving toward his house anyway, as if on autopilot, needing answers.

Chapter 24

It was just about seven and Conrad had set the dining-room table and awaited his guest's arrival. He nervously paced about the large, empty house, wondering if he should be up front with Audrey first or wait till the meal was done and they'd had a glass or two of wine before spilling the beans. Either way, Conrad reconciled himself to the reality that there was no turning back now. Audrey deserved to know he was Grant Pearson's son. And that he held no ill will toward her for what happened to end his father's life. Conrad only wanted to put it past them and work on what they had established these past few weeks.

Hopefully I haven't derailed things to the point that we can't get back on track after I've taken my lumps.

Conrad heard the car pull into his driveway. He tensed, knowing only the truth would set him free. Or send him into a tailspin.

As he pedaled across the hardwood floor toward the foyer, Conrad's leather boots seemed to echo with each rapid beat of his heart. All he could think of was taking Audrey into his arms and kissing her soft lips.

The rest could wait….

He opened the door and, before Conrad was able to take a breath, Audrey stormed past him without saying a word, hands jammed in the deep pockets of her coat.

She rounded on him. The look on her face was one of such fury that Conrad actually flinched.

"What's wrong, Audrey?"

She glared as though looking at a stranger, before Audrey finally willed her mouth to move. "Why didn't you tell me your real name was Ulysses and that you're Grant Pearson's *son?*" she asked through clenched teeth.

Conrad's eyes blinked with shock. How did she find out? *Did it matter at this point?* His secret had been uncovered prematurely.

"I was going to tell you tonight—"

Audrey flashed him a skeptical look. "Yeah, right. You had more than *three* weeks to tell me you were Ulysses Pearson, but chose not to."

"I can explain—"

"Don't bother. You asked me questions about my past and your father, but you already knew the answers. What type of sick game were you playing with me?"

"It was never a game, baby—"

"I'm not *your* baby!" she avowed. "I trusted you, Conrad...or whatever you want to call yourself! I wanted to believe you were different from other men. But you're no damn different, are you? You had your own agenda in cozying up to me and getting me into bed, pretending you were interested in my work and daughter, getting me to fall for you, lying about who you were the whole time."

"It's not what you think, Audrey."

Conrad felt he had climbed into a hole that was getting deeper and more soiled by the moment. Digging his way out of it might take everything he had and then some.

Audrey wanted so badly to give him the benefit of the doubt that what they had was real. But how could she trust what he had to say?

"Just tell me why?" she demanded, hands now planted firmly on small hips. "Why the charade—first at the cemetery and then every other time I saw you?"

Conrad gulped, feeling awkward standing there, an arm's length apart. Audrey looked as if she were in attack mode. Not that he could blame her.

"Let me take your coat and we can sit down—"

When he reached for it, she recoiled as if Conrad were a monster.

"No, *Ulysses!*" Audrey spat, trying to steady her nerves. "I don't plan to stay long. I only came over here because I wanted to get some sort of explanation for what seems like a totally unexplainable thing."

Conrad found himself struggling to look at Audrey, knowing how he must look through her eyes. Suddenly the food that was still simmering seemed little more than an afterthought. He had boxed himself into a corner and he feared that if he didn't do this right he would lose her forever.

He sucked in a deep breath and met Audrey's hard stare. "First of all, Conrad really is my name, albeit middle. I've used it ever since my father died, feeling that Ulysses had died with him, if only in a broken spirit. I came to Festive Cove to try and put some closure to the part of my life that had been most painful. Your painting of my father seemed to bring it all back to me and I needed to somehow reconnect with my past and yours.

"When I first saw you at the cemetery with your daughter, paying respects to the man who had saved your life, I thought it an inappropriate time to just spring myself on you as his long-lost son. The more I got to know you, the more it seemed like a bad idea to disrupt your life and memories by being straight with you. I didn't want to hurt you or Stacy by having you both view me as another victim of a tragic fire that you would forever associate with your own misfortune."

"That doesn't make any sense," Audrey argued. "I'm a big girl, Conrad. In fact, I'm a grown woman and I don't need you or anyone else to decide what I can or can't take."

"I know that," he muttered lamely. "I'm sorry, Audrey. I never intended to hurt you…" *Certainly not in the way I have.*

Her eyes narrowed. "How did you expect me to feel when I found out you had misled me all this time? Happy? Was everything else you portrayed yourself to be one big lie, too?"

Conrad ventured toward her, expecting Audrey to back away. She did not.

"The things that have started to happen between us were never a lie, Audrey, believe me," he said. "You helped me get past the darkness of my past and gave me the strength to carry on. And you made me care for you in a way I never thought I would care for anyone again."

Audrey felt herself soften just a little. "Is that how you show you care—by fabricating your very identity?"

"The only thing I misled you about was not revealing my full name. I really am a single photographer by way of divorce, living in Charleston.

"Was your mother a part of this?"

"She only knew that I came here to see you."

Conrad sighed. "I knew you and I could never really move forward till the whole story came out that we were schoolmates before that Christmas Day tragedy caused our friendship to take a detour that lasted nearly twenty-five years. I swear, that I planned to tell you everything tonight and see if we could get past it."

She fluttered her lashes, still stunned by the unsettling news. "I'm not sure we can. I don't want to be hurt by you anymore."

Conrad swallowed. "You won't be, Audrey. Give me a chance to make it up to you." He ran a hand across her cheek, picking up the moisture from a fallen tear. "I need you. We need each other."

Audrey closed her eyes to the gentleness of his touch. She did need him more than she had needed anyone intimately. It wasn't easy to turn her back on love. But was that enough?

Conrad sensed that he was making headway. He just wanted to see them stay on course for what promised to be a bright future. If only they could put the past behind them.

He lifted Audrey's chin up, forcing her to gaze into his eyes so she could see what he felt inside. "I was never anything but honest about my feelings for you." He spoke sensually and brushed his lips across hers.

Audrey quavered from the kiss, unable to deny what this man was doing to her. She peered deep

into his eyes, looking for a sign of insincerity.
Whether it was an illusion or not, she couldn't find
it.

With her heart skipping a beat, Audrey's lips
parted, urging Conrad forward. He brought his
mouth down hard, attacking her lips like a man possessed. She stood on her tiptoes, kissing him back
just as feverishly, overcome by his redolence.

Conrad pulled Audrey's coat from her shoulders,
tossing it to the floor. He flashed a look of carnal
desire. Seeing the same look on her face, he scooped
her in his arms and carried her up to the bedroom.

They got naked in the blink of an eye, tossing clothes
left and right before falling onto the bed and becoming
entangled in kisses, legs, arms and raw passion.

Audrey went down on Conrad, wishing to please
him this way. She took him in her mouth whole,
wetting and stimulating him with her tongue.

Conrad squeezed his eyes shut and threw his head
back. "Baby, you're making me feel so good."

Too damn good. He wanted her to feel the same.

With a little adjustment of his body, Conrad
managed to put his face between Audrey's long, lean
legs. She was wet and yielded to his tongue. He found
her clitoris and went to town, even as Audrey orally
gratified him, driving them both mad with zeal.

Audrey was sure her climax would come any
moment now even as her tongue whipped back

and forth across the tip of Conrad's erection. She straddled his face with her thighs, feeling his powers of persuasion hitting their mark time and time again.

Conrad gripped her buttocks while Audrey's sweet release came. Only then did he succumb to an orgasm, too, moaning with a violent shudder.

After separating, Conrad wanted only to be inside Audrey. Were they on the same wavelength? Or was it to be oral only?

Audrey answered loud and clear by lying on the bed, legs open and inviting.

"Conrad…" Her voice cried out to him. "Please make love to me now…."

His eyes feasted upon her. "We'll go there to-gether."

Slipping on a condom, Conrad climbed atop Audrey and worked his way inside her. He drove into her powerfully, as she wrapped her legs around him and their bodies, slick with hot perspiration, moved rhythmically nonstop. His chest flattened her breasts but Audrey's nipples remained taut, caressing Conrad even while he stimulated them. Their lips meshed with a kiss so consuming it left Conrad's head spinning.

With her tongue swirling inside Conrad's mouth, Audrey bit down on his lower lip and felt him wince. She arched her back, clinging to him, bracing herself for the explosive result of their lovemaking.

It came with a jolt and erratic breaths as each

fought to the bitter end to achieve every ounce of passionate fulfillment, succeeding in leaps and bounds.

Only after regaining her equilibrium did Audrey wonder if it had been a mistake to give in to temptation. While her love for Conrad was as real as anything she'd ever felt, it was still a puzzle as to who he was at the end of the day. And where he really stood about the past.

Was he really Ulysses, the boy she once knew? Or Conrad, the man Audrey thought she knew?

I certainly can't contemplate this while lying naked in his bed. And now is definitely not the time to talk about a long-distance relationship.

Audrey rolled out of Conrad's arms, as comfortable as they were, and got up in search of her clothes.

Conrad admired her backside and front, too, feeling himself aroused again. He contained this, not wanting to wear the woman out. Or was it the other way around?

"I have to go," she said, ignoring him.

"Can't you stay till we have dinner?" He sat up. "It won't take long to heat up."

"I'm not really hungry, Conrad." Audrey put her bra on.

"You're not still angry with me, are you?"

She sighed. "I don't know what I feel. You kept important facts from me. You misled me. That can't be simply dismissed because of what just happened."

Conrad breathed through his mouth. "I was hoping that precisely because of what just happened, we might be able—"

"We're not kids anymore, *Ulysses*." Audrey's nose crinkled. "We can't kiss and make up and expect everything to be all right."

His mouth hung open. "Excuse me, but I thought that kissing and making up was precisely what we were doing tonight."

"It was just sex," Audrey said tersely, slipping into her dress.

"Ouch." Conrad frowned. "You don't mean that?"

"So maybe it was more than sex," she admitted, though refrained from telling him just how much more it meant to her. "Doesn't change the fact that I'm not sure I can be involved with someone who can't be *completely* honest with me."

Conrad gritted his teeth. "I regret that I wasn't up front about my background from the start. That doesn't change the way I feel about you."

Audrey shot him a wicked gaze. "But it changes the way I feel about you—that's the whole point. Actually, it doesn't, which makes this so frustrating. I don't know *how* I feel right now."

He got to his feet, not wanting to see her walk out of his life. "Can't we at least talk about this?"

"There's nothing more to talk about." She stepped into her shoes. "I just need some time alone."

Conrad felt her slipping from his grasp. He didn't want to give up without a fight.

"Please, Audrey. I know I messed up. It doesn't have to be like this. Let me make it up to you."

She eyed his hard body and then his face, trying to remain steady in her resolve. "I really don't know if that's possible, Conrad."

"All I ask is that you keep an *open* mind."

Audrey jutted her chin. "Did you, when you came up with this masquerade?"

Conrad winced. "That was different."

"Was it really?" She gave him a dubious look. "My advice is the next time you find yourself attracted to a lady, don't pretend to be someone you're not."

"It was never about pretending to be something I wasn't," Conrad insisted. "I only did what I thought was right at the time."

Audrey refused to give in to her own feelings, even if it was killing her. "Why don't we just give it a rest for now and see what happens."

"Nothing will happen if we both aren't of the same mind."

"If it turns out that way, then I guess it just wasn't meant to be."

Audrey didn't necessarily believe that, but she did not want to give him false hope, either. *I love you but I don't like you very much at the moment. This is the only way I know how to deal with it right now.*

Conrad controlled his annoyance, not wishing to add more fuel to a fire of his own making.

He grabbed his pants off the floor. "I'll walk you to the door."

"Please don't," she told him. "I'm sure I can find my own way out."

Conrad stood helplessly as Audrey walked out. With no guarantee she would ever return.

Probably the best thing to ever happen to him now rivaled the worst in how it made him feel. Even sadder was that he didn't know if there was a damned thing he could do about it.

Chapter 25

One of the hardest things Audrey had ever done was to walk away from Conrad. Under the spell of their intense lovemaking, she'd tried to look the other way in ignoring the tremendous letdown. But her hurt rose to the surface. What other choice was there? Conrad had gotten her to open up about a very personal part of her life under false pretenses. She wasn't sure who he really was inside.

The fact that Conrad had turned out to be the son of Grant Pearson was bittersweet to Audrey. She was happy to know Ulysses Pearson had made what seemed to be a fairly good life for himself. That surely had to make Grant proud from the pearly gates of heaven.

But Ulysses had portrayed himself to her as Conrad, photographer, not Conrad, Grant's son.

I wanted so badly for Conrad to be my Prince Charming, insatiable lover and best friend all wrapped up into one. I can't be with a man I can't trust from top to bottom! That wouldn't be fair to me or Stacy.

Audrey shed a few tears while driving as fast as she could without getting into an accident.

Been there, done that with disastrous results. I won't put Stacy through it, either, coloring her future a dark shade of gray.

Dabbing at her eyes, Audrey tried to be strong in the face of weakness where it concerned Conrad and the love she felt for him.

I'm better off without Conrad in my life, confusing me with his two faces and conflicting emotions on his past and the present. I just don't need that type of uncertainty in my life.

She would rather spend another Christmas without male companionship than be with a man who may not truly have her best interests at heart.

Audrey drove around for half an hour to give Stacy more time with Abigail, then picked up her daughter and Mars.

On the way home Audrey tried hard to appear cheerful, but apparently her daughter could see right through her like an open window.

"What's wrong, Mommy?"

"Nothing, honey." She sought to make her voice sound chipper.

"Did you and Conrad get into a fight or something?" Stacy asked.

"Not really, just a little misunderstanding," Audrey said. *More like a huge misunderstanding.*

"Is he coming over for Christmas?"

"I'm not sure about that, sweetheart. Probably not." It was hard for Audrey to say this, knowing Stacy had grown very fond of Conrad. So had she, till realizing that all the glitter about him was something less than pure gold.

"But I thought you liked Conrad?" Stacy's tone was sad. "And he liked you."

Audrey glanced in the rearview mirror at her. "I do like him, honey, but right now I like him more as a friend. Conrad has his own life in Charleston and I think it's a good idea that we don't get too attached to him."

"But I thought we already were?"

Audrey forced a smile through the wall of despair at her daughter's insightfulness. *How do I explain that I knew Conrad as Ulysses when I was your age, but only learned that tonight?*

She decided it was best not to tarnish Stacy's good memories of Conrad.

"If so, then maybe we should take a step backward and try to focus more on the life you and I have together. I'd say it's a pretty good one. Wouldn't you?"

"I guess," muttered Stacy. "At least Conrad left us with Mars, if he doesn't plan to spend any more time with us."

Thank goodness for small favors, Audrey thought. Stacy had grown quite attached to Mars. Too bad his former owner turned out to be just another dishonest man with his own agenda.

A man who Audrey happened to be in love with.

Chapter 26

"That's quite a story," Brandon said over the phone.

"Yeah, and not a very good one at the moment." Conrad sat in the darkened living room with a glass of wine, feeling depressed and disillusioned. He had called his best friend and told the whole tale, right down to Audrey walking out on him—maybe for good.

"Audrey must be some special lady to have you running around in circles like this."

Conrad pursed his lips. "She is. There's no doubt about it. I never thought in a million years I'd end up falling in love with someone in Festive Cove; much less the girl my dad saved."

"And obviously she feels something for you, too, even if it may border on hate at the moment."

"I don't think Audrey could hate me right now any more than I hate myself."

"I've never known you to give up on something so easily, Conrad. It doesn't have to be over."

"She made it abundantly clear that trusting me ever again is going to be a long shot at best. Not sure we'll be able to get past this."

"Maybe you can. But only if you don't throw in the towel, only to end up regretting it for the rest of your life."

"So what do you suggest?" Conrad wet his lips with wine.

"That's simple. Fight for her, man. Yeah, you screwed up big-time. But it happens—especially when you went there with a totally different agenda than romancing this gorgeous artist and falling in love."

That agenda was something Conrad dreaded to even think about. No longer did he wish to confront Audrey about his father's death. Now he just wanted to make her realize that it wasn't about that anymore. It was about them and second chances.

Had he blown a golden opportunity to find true happiness with someone with guts, talent and love to give?

He said his goodbyes to Brandon when Conrad heard the doorbell ring. Might Audrey have had a change of heart? The mere possibility warmed his insides. If only she could let bygones be bygones, then the sky was definitely the limit for them.

He opened the door to find Willis standing there.

"I tried phoning, but I kept getting your voice mail," Willis said.

Conrad welcomed him in, though not especially in the mood for company. "Can I get you a drink?"

"Yeah, sure."

"Is wine all right?"

Willis nodded, following Conrad as he grabbed his own glass before heading to the kitchen.

"You alone?"

Conrad gave him a blank stare. *I wish I could say otherwise.* "Nobody here but me."

"I think I blew it," Willis said after he took the wine.

Conrad cocked a brow. "What are you talking about?"

"Audrey Lamour." Willis tasted the wine. "We ran into each other at a mutual friend's house. Audrey talked about having dinner with a friend. I kind of mentioned the whole deal regarding your coming to the station, your dad and asking about her. It took me a while to realize what was going on. I had no clue you were holding back on some things for whatever reason…"

Conrad frowned and sipped his wine. "How could you have known?"

Christmas Heat

"Sorry about that."

"It's all right. She was going to find out sooner or later." *Why couldn't it have been a little later when I told her myself?*

Willis scratched his cheek. "I take it Audrey was here?"

"Yes."

"What happened?"

Conrad thought of their passionate lovemaking, which he'd wanted to believe would put them back on track. Instead it appeared to have had the opposite effect. He wouldn't go so far as to say that men and women were from different worlds, but Conrad was disappointed that things had ended up as they had.

"Let's just say that we had a falling out of sorts and I'm definitely in the doghouse as far as Audrey's concerned."

Finding a way out would be one of Conrad's greatest challenges.

Chapter 27

It was Christmas Eve and Conrad found himself trying to act as if he could take or leave Audrey. It couldn't be further from the truth. He had no desire to see their relationship come to an end. Not without attempting to make things right between them. But how? Audrey seemed in no mood to discuss it last night. Why should today be any different?

Why shouldn't it? It's worth a try to convince her that I am no fraud when it comes to how I feel about her and Stacy.

It was just after 3:00 p.m. Conrad had decided to pack most of his things. He planned to head back to Charleston tomorrow, should things remain frosty between him and Audrey. He wasn't crazy about traveling on Christmas Day. Who would be? As things stood, he didn't want to hang around to mourn his father's death on Christmas along with the demise of what Conrad thought was the makings of a concrete relationship with Audrey.

No matter what name I used, it doesn't change my feelings for her one bit. I love Audrey for everything she is as a woman, mother, artist and human being.

And he loved Audrey's daughter because Stacy was part of her mother and a bright, sweet little girl in her own right.

I don't want to lose them. But is it out of my hands?

Conrad stood up and, walking to the window, stared out at Mother Nature and all her glory at this time of year as snowflakes flittered through the air, floating down to the ground. He searched for answers that made sense, but came up empty-handed.

Is this really the way it has to be? Or do You have something else in mind to save the day before it's too late and I lose Audrey forever?

Audrey had spent the last couple of hours working on the painting of Grant, tweaking it here and there, filling in the blanks, adding more hues and depth.

Unfortunately now she could also see a little bit of Conrad in him. The man who had stolen her heart and given her a new reason to live. Only to snatch it away.

Could they work things out in time? Or would the trust issue always come between them?

That afternoon, Audrey and Stacy took Mars for a walk. Fresh snow formed a thin layer over the sidewalk and lawns, while earlier snowfall sat in clumps here and there like little pyramids. Mars, restless as he was, clearly did not like being confined to a leash. Audrey imagined him and Stacy running free someday in a big grassy field behind their house. But for now they had to deal with both the limitations of small-town life and with a big city's traffic nightmares, which could be detrimental to a dog's safety.

"Merry Christmas," Audrey said cheerfully with a wave to neighbors who poked their heads out or were scraping ice off car windows. She got the same greeting in return.

She was glad that Christmas was less than twenty-four hours away, deciding it was better to get this year's holiday over and done with as soon as possible. Aside from reminding her that it was the anniversary of the day her parents died, Audrey knew that Conrad would also be reliving his father's death and remembering that Grant had given his life after saving hers.

Does Conrad somehow hold that against me? Is that what the pretense was really all about? Did he only want to get into my head while clearing his own?

Audrey stiffened at the thought. The truth was

she had always felt guilty that Grant Pearson's family had been left to suffer with his death, leaving them without a husband and father. But Audrey's loss was no less painful, if not more. She wasn't to blame for the fire that changed their lives. Conrad had no right to keep the truth from her. No matter how hard his own painful memories were.

What was he thinking?

Audrey watched Stacy and Mars ahead of her as they neared home. Maybe it was best she didn't know. It would only make her more upset that she had let her guard down and been stung by Conrad's deception. So maybe he was attracted to her on some level, but it came with strings attached. Whereas her own interest in him had been heartfelt and unconditional.

Audrey considered how different physically the man Conrad was from the boy Ulysses she knew. Conrad had matured into a very fit Adonis. Yet, the resemblance was clearly there now that she realized they were one and the same.

Audrey stopped in her tracks when she saw Conrad enthusiastically greeting Stacy and Mars.

He watched them approach as a loving family at Christmastime and Conrad felt a knot in his stomach at the prospect that he might never get to continue their relationship or possibly make them his own family. It was Mars who first ran up to him, seemingly overjoyed at seeing his short-term owner again.

Conrad was equally happy to see him, petting the dog while saying, "So you missed me, too, huh, Mars?"

Then Stacy gave him a thousand-watt smile. "Hi, Conrad."

"Hey there, Stacy." He grinned back, putting a hand on her shoulder.

"I thought we wouldn't see you anymore," she said soberly.

Conrad hid his displeasure at the idea, fearing that it had already begun to take effect on Stacy.

"There was no chance of that," he told her. "I'd never leave without saying goodbye."

"I wish you didn't have to leave at all." Stacy pouted and kicked at snow with her boot.

"So do I," Conrad said sourly. *More than you could ever know. But it is what it is, through no fault of yours.* "Unfortunately, I have a life in Charleston to get back to." *And it seems as if I've worn out my welcome here. At least with your mother.*

As Audrey approached the group, she felt sadness deep in her soul. Having heard Conrad indicate that he was leaving seemed to bring the finality of their brief but painful separation and his deceit to a whole new level. Though she wanted with all her heart to try and patch things up with Conrad, Audrey felt that they might have reached a point of no return, all things considered.

"Hello, Audrey." Conrad spoke formally, as if they were veritable strangers.

"Conrad," she responded in a monotone as Stacy and Mars looked on, starry-eyed.

He tried to read her mind. Maybe there was hope yet they could get past this.

"Do you think we could talk inside?"

Her first instinct was to say no, as Audrey didn't wish to rehash his lame explanation for misleading her. Or think of him in romantic terms anymore, as difficult as that was. But a part of her didn't want to believe this was the end of them.

I have to at least hear him out. Don't I?

"Yes, just for a few minutes." Audrey averted her gaze, turning to Stacy. "Why don't you and Mars play out here for a little while? But stay in front of the house."

"Okay," Stacy agreed. She flashed Conrad a hopeful smile and ran toward a mound of snow with Mars close behind.

Chapter 28

They stood in the living room. Audrey considered asking Conrad to sit down and offering him coffee. But right now she was in no mood to make things comfortable as though he were still Conrad, the man she had fallen in love with, instead of Ulysses Conrad Pearson, someone who was almost a stranger to her.

Conrad couldn't help but think how lovely Audrey looked and how he wanted nothing more than to take her in his arms, declare his undying love and live happily thereafter. Except this was no fairy tale.

If only things could go back to how they were for them before his true identity came to light. *Why did I wait so long to be straight with her?*

She met his eyes coldly. "So talk…"

This was more difficult than Conrad had imagined, sharing more of his past that he'd kept from her and all others. If there was to be any chance of repairing the damage he'd done to them, he had to go for it.

He took a breath as if a trigger for speaking his mind, in telling a tale a quarter of a century in the making.

"Twenty-five years ago, I had a dream about my father being trapped inside a burning house. When I woke up in a cold sweat, I thought it was all in my head. That's when I learned that my father had been called to a house fire that early Christmas morning. I had a really bad feeling that my dream had been a nightmarish omen. I begged him not to go, but Daddy said he had to do his job as a firefighter.

"I stood by helplessly with my mother and watched him leave, knowing deep down inside that I would never see my father alive again. And I didn't." Conrad choked back the words, his gaze focused on her face. "Since then, a part of me has blamed myself for not stopping him from dying, even when I knew Daddy did what he had to. It just wasn't enough. For a time, I even felt that God should have done something to stop the flames from engulfing three innocent people. Of course, I know now it doesn't work that way."

Audrey put herself in Conrad's shoes, feeling as if she could relate on so many levels, including casting blame where there was none.

Conrad sensed that he had at least gotten Audrey's attention in baring his soul. That was a step in the right direction. Maybe she would ease up and relate to him again as a man who truly cared for her.

"I suppose I never really dealt with what happened in the right way," he reflected. "After I read about you in the magazine and saw what you'd done with the photograph my mother gave you, it seemed time to come back to Festive Cove and face my demons head-on."

Audrey arched her brows. "Why didn't you just tell me all this from the *very* beginning?" she asked, dismissing his earlier reasoning as vague and unsatisfactory.

Conrad pinched the bridge of his nose. "Believe me, I wanted to. But the timing never seemed quite right. The more I got to know you as a woman, the harder it became to want to look back at us as kids and go down that road. I didn't want to hurt you more than you already had been by bringing up the devastating consequences of the fire."

"Did you think that hiding behind a fake person pretending to be a real one wouldn't hurt me?" Her lashes batted. "I fell in love with you and you were dishonest with me...."

Conrad winced, hearing the word *love* come from her lips for the first time. He'd suspected as much, given that Conrad felt the same emotion, growing steadily over the past three weeks. His reluctance to

tell Audrey the truth about his past was based on uncertainty of how it would impact their feelings for
each other. As well as his own uncertainty about
himself.

"I wasn't thinking right," he told her lamely. "I
was trying to protect you from everything we both
went through, without your reliving it each time you
saw my face. And I was a mess. I had no idea how I
truly felt about being back here and facing the past.
It was a dumb thing to do, I realize now. I'm really
sorry about that, Audrey. For both of us."

"So am I," Audrey said, wishing this weren't so
hard. "Sorry that you didn't trust me enough to let
me form my own opinion of you and what you were
going through."

She was sorry, too, that he didn't allow them a
real chance to get to know each other for who they
really were.

Most of all, Audrey was sorry that she still
couldn't be sure just how much of Conrad's feelings
for her were real and how much were simply a part
of the alter ego he'd created.

Conrad wanted to kiss Audrey, longing to taste her
sweet, moist lips. He didn't dare act upon that desire.
Not this time. Not till he knew they were back on
track.

"Where do we go from here?" he asked hesitantly.

Audrey sighed. "I'm not sure what you want me
to say, Conrad."

"Say what you feel."

"I just wish things had taken a different turn. I would've preferred to get to know the *real* you."

"You did, baby," he insisted, thumping his chest. "The part of me in here."

She planted a hand on her hip. "I'm sorry but I don't see it that way."

"Everything I've told you about my life in general and feelings for you were absolutely true. And I don't think it's unreasonable for me to have wanted you to know me for who I am—not for who my father was and our shared tragedy."

Audrey remained silent as minutes ticked by.

"Well, I guess I've said what I came to say. I'm sorry I made some mistakes with us. Wish I could do things over, but I can't. The one thing I never claimed was to be perfect. I'm not."

"I never wanted perfection from you, Conrad," Audrey insisted, knowing there was no such thing. "Only an honest man I could trust."

"You can trust me."

If only I could believe that. Problem was, she needed trust in actions and not merely words. On that score Conrad had failed miserably.

"I'm not sure I can." She spoke honestly, rejecting every bone in her body that told Audrey that he was worth a second chance. At this point she felt she would be better safe than sorry.

Conrad wanted to press on, try his best to convince Audrey that he was honest, by and large, and could definitely be trusted to do right by her and Stacy. It all seemed too little, too late now.

"I'll be leaving tomorrow," he said quietly.

Audrey's left brow shot up. *So soon?* Had she honestly expected him to stick it out till the New Year and beyond? What would have been the point?

"Why Christmas Day?" she asked, as if he needed a reason.

"Why not?" Conrad's voice had an edge to it. "There seems to be nothing more for me here. Or is there?"

Audrey bit her lip. Should she backpedal and say something to get him to stay? But what?

"I won't stand in your way if you want to go."

He took a breath. "What I want, Audrey, is for us to work things out."

"It's not that simple," she said, wishing otherwise.

"Nothing ever is."

Audrey choked back tears. *I don't want to put all my faith in Conrad again, only to be let down again.*

"I should check on Stacy and Mars," she told him, for lack of a better response.

Conrad frowned. "I guess it's goodbye then," he said reluctantly. "Merry Christmas, Audrey."

Tongue-tied, Audrey watched as Conrad walked out the door and likely out of her life forever. For a moment she was frozen, caught between the desire to go after him and the reluctance to do so for fear of surrendering her feelings once more. Audrey couldn't bear the thought of being hurt again, perhaps irrevocably, by someone she had grown to care for.

She chose to believe that what was meant to be would be. Even if Conrad was no longer a part of her life.

Chapter 29

With his time in Festive Cove running out and any chance of a continuing relationship with Audrey apparently over, Conrad found himself parked in front of the one place that had once been his comfort zone: the home he grew up in. It was decorated in flashing red, blue and green Christmas lights and seemed to be inviting him to come inside.

Not as if I have anywhere else to go. Other than an empty house with no Christmas cheer.

Conrad left the car and made his way across a walkway of snowy footprints to the front door. He was having second thoughts, even as he rang the bell.

A young man opened the door, regarding him quizzically.

Too late to run away now. Conrad found he no longer wanted to.

"Hi. My name's Conrad Pearson. I used to live here. I was just passing through the old neighborhood and that down-memory-lane thing hit me."

The man cocked a brow but said nothing.

"You think I could come in for just a few minutes?" Conrad asked tentatively. *Hope he doesn't think I'm out to cause trouble.* "I know it's probably asking a lot of a stranger—"

"You're welcome to check out the place," he told him in a friendly voice. "I'm Sonny Byrd."

Conrad shook his hand. "I appreciate this."

"No problem. Nice to know that some people never forget where they came from."

Conrad was introduced to Sonny's wife, Priscilla. She was holding a baby boy who favored his father.

They allowed Conrad to take a look around. He soaked up the tour like a sponge, displacing current images with distant ones present only in the deep corners of his mind. The house was smaller than Conrad remembered, but equally warm and inviting. He felt a great sense of belonging.

"Do you have any children, Conrad?" Priscilla asked.

In my dreams. "I haven't been that blessed thus far."

"You don't know what you're missing, man," Sonny stated as an authority. Now holding his son, he kissed him for effect.

"I can see that." Conrad looked at them enviously. He thought about what it would be like to become Stacy's father, while he and Audrey produced several more of their own children down the line. If only things had turned out differently.

Conrad went out to his car and came back with one of the landscapes Audrey had painted, having given the other one to Willis and his family for Christmas. Though he loved the paintings dearly as a reflection of the artist, Conrad had decided they would be too painful a reminder of what he had lost in Audrey the woman. He would still present the portrait of himself to his mother, knowing it would be well received.

"This is for you," Conrad told the Byrds, much to their surprise. "A good friend of mine painted it. I suggest you hold on to it, as it will be even more valuable someday."

"It's beautiful," Priscilla gushed. "Thank you so much, Conrad. God bless you!"

"You, too. Merry Christmas!" Conrad gave a broad smile and thanked them for their hospitality, before making his way to the place he'd called a temporary home for one last night.

It was a quarter past ten and Stacy was already in bed with Mars, waiting for Christmas morning and Santa Claus's certain arrival with plenty of gifts. Audrey welcomed the downtime between then and now, enjoying some hot chocolate in the breakfast room with Regina. She had given her friend a full rundown on the situation with Conrad.

"Wow, is all I have to say," Regina voiced dramatically over her mug. "Or maybe *weird* is more like it. I just can't believe Conrad is the *same* Ulysses you knew in grade school—the boy whose firefighter dad rescued you from your burning house."

"It threw me for a loop, too," Audrey admitted, and that was putting it mildly. "I never imagined that Ulysses would grow up to become the likes of Conrad: the good, bad and everything in between."

"He's going back to Charleston tomorrow?" Regina asked.

"Looks that way." Audrey sipped her cocoa thoughtfully.

"And you're just going to let him go and let what you have slip away just like that?"

"You mean, what we *had*," Audrey emphasized. "Conrad misled me, Regina, pure and simple. I've had enough of dishonest men in my life. I don't need to be with someone who can so easily keep such a big secret."

Regina played with her long amethyst-polished nails. "Maybe you're being too hard on him, girl. I mean, put yourself in his position, hard as that may be. His father died trying to save your parents' lives after rescuing you from the flames. Then Conrad shows up in town and sees you for the first time in person at his dad's gravesite. If he had started talking to you then, you probably would've freaked out."

Audrey's nose wrinkled. "Even if I agreed with that, Conrad could have told me who he was when he came to my house the next day. Or anytime afterward when he knew that we were starting to get close. But I had to find out through Willis. Can you imagine how that made me feel?"

Regina shifted on the stool. "All I'm saying, Audrey, is I think you need to talk about it with Conrad some more, instead of retreating into your shell. I'll grant you it wasn't Conrad's smartest move to keep his real identity from you. But I'm telling you that the man's heart is still in the right place. He really cares for you, no matter what name he used or what happened to change both of your lives. And you *love* him, girlfriend, even if you wish it weren't true."

"But that's just it, I don't wish that," Audrey said, frustrated. "I'd like nothing more than for this deception to have never happened and instead have us both to be professing our love for one another over and over. But this obviously wasn't part of God's plan for me."

"Says who?" Regina's gaze sharpened. "If you ask me, I think God brought you two together, Audrey. Even if He may sometimes work in mysterious ways. Don't you see, He's taken you two full circle in your lives and is now testing your mettle under adversity. It's up to you to get past the half-

truths and mistrust and give Mr. Ulysses Conrad
Pearson a chance to make things right."

Audrey downed more hot chocolate. *Was that
truly Your plan, God? Did You really mean for
Conrad and me to meet again years later and
survive trust issues to become seriously involved? Or
is Regina way off base and what You really want is
for us to go our separate ways while we still can?*

Audrey didn't wait for an answer. "I just think that
we both need some space right now," she suggested
as a compromise. "Maybe after the holidays are over
and things settle down, Conrad and I can talk."

"Yeah, but will you?" Regina gave her a straight
look. "The man's flying back to Charleston tomorrow.
What if by not talking now, you lose him forever?"

"Then I guess it wouldn't have been God's plan
that we hook up after all, would it?"

Audrey doubted her own words, even if they
seemed logical. Truthfully, she didn't know what to
think anymore where it concerned Conrad. Yes, he
was almost everything she could want, romantically
speaking. But she needed more than that to commit
to him or anyone else. Right now she just wanted to
be there for her daughter on Christmas Day and try
and enjoy it for Stacy.

Even if in the back of Audrey's mind, the specter
of Christmas past would always be there. As she
knew it would be for Conrad.

Chapter 30

Conrad unlocked his eyes, a slow but persistent moan erupting from his throat. His heart was pounding like a hammer and, for an instant, he wasn't quite sure where he was. But as his vision adjusted to the dark of night, Conrad realized he was in bed. A glance at the digital clock atop the dresser told him that it was 4:00 a.m. on Christmas Day.

He'd been dreaming that there was a fire at Audrey's house. She and Stacy had been trapped and he had been attempting to save them. Just as his father had sought to save Audrey and her parents twenty-five years ago this morning.

Conrad dismissed it as nothing more than a nightmare, given the day and place. But what if it was more than that? What if this was meant to warn him of an impending tragedy?

A sense of dread came over Conrad as he assessed the possibility that Audrey and Stacy were actually in real danger. He didn't want to believe that Audrey's house could really be on fire simply because he dreamed it. Or maybe his dream was a true nightmare in the making....

Conrad jumped out of bed and grabbed his cell phone off the night table. He rang Audrey's number. The phone rang three times, before her voice mail picked up.

"Hi, I'm either away, busy or both. If you leave a message, I'll try to get back to you as quickly as possible. Have a nice day and happy holidays! Bye-bye."

"Audrey, this is Conrad." His voice shook. "If you're there, please pick up the phone...."

He waited anxiously for her to do so, needing to know that everything was fine. But she did not come onto the line. Probably because she was sound asleep at this hour.

Or it could be she was hurt and unable to get to the phone. The fire might have already trapped them.

Going with his gut instincts, Conrad dialed Willis's number.

After four rings, a sleepy voice answered. "Do you know what time it is...?"

"I need your help." Conrad spoke with a tone of desperation. "I think that Audrey's house may be on fire."

"You think? Or you *know?*"

Conrad considered his answer for a moment. The last thing he wanted was for Willis to think him crazy in calling about a fire Conrad had only his dream to vouch for.

"I know," he told him firmly. "Look, I'll explain later. Can you call 9-1-1, the fire department, whatever it takes to get your people over to her house in a hurry—please?"

Willis breathed into the phone. "All right, Conrad, but this had better be the real deal."

"It is." Conrad felt certain Audrey, Stacy and Mars were in trouble. "I'm going over there right now. I'll see you."

"Don't try to be a hero, Conrad." Willis's voice hardened. "Leave the firefighting to the fire department—"

"I'll do what I need to protect those I care about."

Conrad disconnected on that note. He wasn't interested in being a hero, only in saving the woman he loved and her daughter. The thought of them being overcome by flames like Conrad's father and Audrey's parents had been was too much to stomach.

Conrad quickly threw on his clothes and was running out the door in one continuous motion. He tried Audrey's number again and got no answer, making him even more apprehensive as to what he would find when he got there.

Audrey was sleeping soundly. But this was intruded upon by a dream that transported her back in time to when she was seven years old. She was trapped in her bedroom by flames that pierced through her closed door like fiery daggers. She could hear her parents screaming her name, as if the only way to reach her.

"Momma, Daddy…" she called out to them, knowing that they, too, were ensnared by the inferno engulfing their house.

"We love you, baby," her mother shouted. "God will take care of you for us."

"No, Momma, I don't want Him to. Not without you and Daddy."

Audrey had the feeling that her words had fallen on deaf ears. The thick cloudlike smoke made it all but impossible to see and she began to feel light-headed.

Opening her eyes, Audrey heard the smoke detectors screaming. She immediately lifted to one elbow in bed, noting it was just after four in the morning. She smelled smoke.

The house was on fire.

Getting up, Audrey grabbed her robe and ran into the hall, seeing nothing unusual. She took a couple of steps down the stairwell and, glancing over the banister, saw flames below shooting up from the living room like fireworks. Panic whizzed through Audrey.

Fearing that Stacy had gone downstairs to open her Christmas gifts, Audrey raced to her daughter's room. She breathed a huge sigh of relief when she saw Stacy sound asleep in bed, oblivious to what was happening.

Audrey shook Stacy, resolving to keep calm. "Wake up, honey."

Stacy made a humming sound, but was still almost drugged in her deep sleep.

Audrey nudged her harder. "Come on, sweetheart, open your eyes. We have to get out of here."

As if her words finally registered, Stacy opened her eyes. "What's wrong, Mommy?"

"There's a fire in the living room, honey. We have to get out of the house now."

Stacy rubbed her eyes, sitting up. "Where's Mars?"

"I don't know," Audrey said. "Maybe downstairs…"

The thought that the dog may have somehow started the fire and could be hurt alarmed her, but she couldn't let Stacy see this.

Just then, Mars came into the room and hopped up on the bed, barking wildly like a dog high on meth. Stacy held on to him for dear life.

"Don't worry, boy," Stacy uttered bravely. "I won't let the fire hurt you."

"Let me have him for now," Audrey said, taking the dog. "Throw on your robe, Stacy, and hurry!"

A couple of minutes later, they made it out of the house safe and sound, negotiating tracks of fire that had seemed to spread in every direction like a fast-moving epidemic.

Waiting outside with curious neighbors for the fire department to arrive, Audrey watched helplessly as the first floor of her house was immersed in flames. It brought back memories of her childhood and the Christmas Day fire. The thought chilled Audrey's bones. How could it happen twice in one lifetime? She could only thank God that the end result had turned out differently this time. Both she and her daughter had been spared and would live to see another day.

Audrey had an arm around Stacy, who was holding Mars, as though he was one of her dolls. Then, inexplicably, Stacy set the dog down and bolted toward the house.

"Stacy!" Audrey screamed. "Stop!"

"I forgot something," her daughter said frantically. Mars chased after her barking.

"Don't go back into the house, young lady!" Audrey ordered her. But the words were ignored as Stacy and Mars sprinted inside the burning house.

Audrey's heart pounded as she went after her daughter, pedaling across the snow-covered lawn toward the front door.

Conrad could see the flames painting the house sharp tones of yellow, red and blue even from a distance. By the time he pulled up in front, the blazing colors were even more vivid and alarming. He saw the onlookers milling about like zombies. In the middle of the crowd were Audrey, Stacy and Mars.

Thank God no one appears to be hurt, Conrad thought, even if the place they called home looked as if it would suffer serious damage, if not be totally lost.

Then to his horror, Conrad watched as Stacy let Mars slip out of her arms while breaking free of Audrey's grasp and running back toward the house. Mars was in hot pursuit, seemingly undeterred by the blaze that threatened to taken them both.

It was the nightmare Conrad had dreamt about. He stared with disbelief, leaving him feeling frightened and bewildered. Only this time he was wide-awake and could do something about it. He would not let that little girl, or her mother, in trying to save her, die a horrible death, so help him God.

Conrad sprang from the car, pushing his way past people as if they weren't there. He grabbed hold of Audrey just before she could enter the house.

"I'll get them," he promised her.

But Audrey, hysterical, did not seem to fully grasp this. "Let me go," she screamed. "My baby's in there!"

He held on to her firmly. "I know. Don't worry, I'll go—"

"I don't know what I'd do if Stacy were hurt or—"

Conrad made Audrey look at him. "I won't let anything happen to Stacy, I promise. Just wait here for the fire department to arrive. Please, Audrey."

Audrey was trembling as she honed in on Conrad's face. Where had he come from?

"All right," she told him. "But *please* hurry!"

Conrad nodded. "I'll be back," he said. "We'll all come out safe and sound!"

Conrad prayed he could deliver on this assurance, knowing full well anything less would haunt him for the rest of his life.

Audrey wiped away tears as she put faith in Conrad and God to save her daughter and Mars. She felt neighbors pulling her back from the house while Conrad ran inside, seemingly ignoring the relentless flames that were determined to block his path.

Chapter 31

There were pockets of fire between thick plumes of smoke. Conrad made his way through almost blindly, not sure where Stacy and Mars had gone. Or why they had come back in. His first guess was that she had reentered the house to get a doll or something. Kids tended to place value in items out of proportion to their significance under such dire conditions. What was important was finding Stacy before the blaze became too hot to handle, the smoke too suffocating and the house a tinderbox from which there was no escape.

"Stacy!" Conrad yelled. "Can you hear me?" His worst fear was that she had already been overcome by the smoke and was lying unconscious, unable to communicate her whereabouts.

Then he heard her voice, muffled by the crackling sound of flames.

"Help us!"

"Where are you, Stacy?" Conrad called out. His lungs were starting to feel the sting from the putrid smoke flooding the house like poisonous vapors.

"We're upstairs," she cried. "Please hurry."

"I'm coming, honey. Hold on."

Conrad mounted the stairs two at a time. He made his way through the dense smoke and flames, before reaching Stacy's room. There was no sign of her or Mars.

"Stacy!" Conrad called out.

"We're in Mommy's room," she cried out.

He found the girl and dog huddled together on the floor in a corner. The smoke was not as thick in the room, though small patches of fire were springing up as a prelude to an all out inferno. Conrad rushed to them.

"Are you all right?" he asked Stacy, who looked terrified but otherwise unharmed.

"Yeah, and so is Mars." The dog barked while staying close to Stacy as if to protect her. "Are we going to die?"

Conrad regarded her sympathetically, seeing Audrey in a similar situation many years ago.

"No, you're not. My dad saved your mother once

upon a time from the fire and I'm here to do the same thing for you."

Stacy's eyes widened with fascination. "Grant's *your* daddy?"

"Yeah, and the *best* fireman there ever was." Conrad gave her a warm and pensive smile. "We can talk about it later. Right now, we have to get out of here." He gently lifted the girl up. She held on to Mars.

"Wait." Stacy turned toward a covered canvas up against the wall. "You've got to bring the painting, Conrad!"

"No time for any of that," he said dismissively, even if Conrad knew how difficult it would be for Audrey to see her hard work go up in flames.

"We have to!" Stacy insisted. "Mommy has to have it for Christmas. She finished the painting of Grant. He was her guardian angel. Now you're mine, Conrad. Please—"

Conrad was surprised at her conviction in saving the portrait for Audrey. He lifted the cover and was surprised to see that the painting was now complete. It was similar to the one at the firehouse, yet strikingly different. Audrey had added new dimensions and vibrant colors, making a true masterpiece. Conrad imagined she planned to hang it in her bedroom as another tribute to his father.

He put the cover back over the painting and grabbed it with one hand, holding Stacy firmly with the other. "Okay, let's go!"

"I'm scared," sobbed Stacy, trembling.

"Don't be." Conrad tried to reassure her. "Together we have to be brave and we'll get out of this alive. After all, you want your mother to keep her painting of Dad. And an even better gift will be her knowing you're safe and sound for Christmas, don't you think?"

"Yes," she said meekly.

Conrad sensed a new degree of determination in the girl to survive, matching his own.

"Put this cloth over your nose and mouth and breathe slowly," he instructed. "And whatever you do, don't let Mars go."

"I won't."

They retraced Conrad's path and hurried down the stairs. The fire had begun to spread toward Audrey's studio. Conrad knew how dangerous that could be with all the flammable liquids she handled. He could hear the screaming sirens of the fire engines on the scene and knew that help was on the way. But would it be too late?

Keeping Stacy and the painting close to his body, Conrad guided them through the flames, feeling searing heat licking at his face. He ignored this, as his father had a quarter of a century before, wanting only to save three lives and be able to talk about it for years to come.

They came out the door and Conrad immediately felt the welcome cold air hit his face like a slap.

Firefighters descended upon them like vultures, moving them away from the house.

The first face Conrad saw was Audrey's, as Stacy ran into her arms.

"What were you thinking, honey?" Audrey demanded, trying to balance her anger and fear and relief.

"I'm sorry, Mommy. I had to keep the painting from being lost forever."

"Painting…?" Audrey's mind was a blur, so happy that they had all made it out alive and well. She gazed at Conrad, who looked weary with soot in patches all over his face. He was holding one of her paintings.

"Your guardian angel," he said evenly, and lifted the cover off to reveal Grant Pearson. The painting had been unharmed. "Looks like your daughter was on a mission, just like my old man was back in the day."

Audrey wept, thinking that Grant truly was her guardian angel. For he had sent his son to give her back her daughter, saving them both from a fate neither deserved.

She admired the portrait that had managed to withstand the fire as if by divine intervention.

Thank you, God, for giving me the blessings this Christmas that truly mean the most.

Blessings Audrey would never forget. Starting with the timely reemergence of Conrad in her world, as though they were destined to continue to be an important part of each other's lives in spite of themselves.

Audrey noted now that he was wincing in discomfort and saw that Conrad's hands were burned.

"You're hurt," she said with an intake of breath.

"It's no big deal. Strictly superficial." Conrad half smiled, her presence dulling the pain more than Audrey knew. "I'd say your house is in much worse shape."

They both looked up at the structure that the firefighters were desperately trying to salvage.

Audrey hated the thought of losing her home, her studio and so many precious memories. But she had gone down that path before. She would gladly trade in her home for the lives of those she cared about most.

She turned to Conrad Pearson, the corners of her lips curving upward gratefully.

Chapter 32

"You knew about the fire before anyone else?" Audrey looked at Conrad as he lay in a hospital bed, bandages covering his hands. His burns were expected to heal completely.

Conrad contemplated the question while feeling the effects of the painkillers kicking in. "Yes, I suppose I did."

"But how?"

He'd asked himself the same question and wasn't sure what the answer was—other than that it was somehow meant to be. "Came in a dream—weird, huh?"

"Not in my book."

Audrey's eyes twinkled. She had a feeling that Grant was watching over them from heaven.

Conrad shifted his position so he could more comfortably see Audrey's beautiful face. "Maybe there was a reason for everything we've been through for the past twenty-five years. My guess is that we were supposed to work our way to each other at the end of the day—even if there were some bumps in the road. I'm just sorry it had to come down to the fire and my poor decision making in not being up front with you from the start."

"Neither of us were responsible for the fire, Conrad." Audrey gazed at him. "The fire investigators suspect Mars might have accidentally caused the Christmas tree to somehow ignite." She thanked God the fire had been contained before it spread to her studio and before it had caused irreparable damage to the house's structure. "As for poor decision making, I think we both made some mistakes."

She refused to put all the blame on him insofar as the twists and turns their relationship had taken. Not anymore. Audrey now had a whole new perspective on her life and times, as well as Conrad's.

Destiny truly has shone upon us. Here we are together as the ultimate survivors with some stories to tell.

To Conrad this was as good a time as any to put his heart out there and hope it wasn't too little, too late.

"One very big mistake I made, Audrey, was not telling you a lot sooner than now that I've fallen in love with you. Guess I needed to see if the curtain had dropped on our relationship once you knew my true identity. At this stage I see no reason to hold back any longer, even if the love you felt for me has diminished with everything that's happened."

The words made Audrey want to melt on the spot, if not in Conrad's arms. The austere confines of a hospital room hardly seemed like the right place for one to profess love. Or receive it. Yet somehow this seemed perfectly appropriate, given their shared history of turning tragedy into triumph.

"I love you, too, Conrad," she freely admitted, knowing it had been hard, if not impossible, to fall out of love with him. He had proven himself to be a man worthy of such love when it came down to crunch time. "Or should I start calling you *Ulysses* from this point on?"

He grinned. "Conrad is good. But call me whatever you want if that's what it takes to get you and Stacy into my life permanently."

She grinned. "I'll stick with Conrad, since I've gotten used to it."

"Well I hope you get used to it a lot more."

"I want that, too." Audrey wondered what the future

held for them. Yes, they loved each other and seemed in sync by and large. But there was still the fact that they lived thousands of miles apart and they had not exactly bridged that gap as yet. "About us—"

Conrad checked her with a lift of his hand, ignoring the slight discomfort. "I don't want there to be the slightest doubt on your part, Audrey, as to making a commitment to spend the rest of your life with me. While I'm definitely my father's son, I'd rather not be seen as a hero or someone you're obliged to for saving Stacy's life."

"I have no doubts about what I feel for you, Conrad," Audrey told him. "I'll *always* be indebted to you for coming through the way you did, but I don't want to be with you as my hero. Your father, bless his soul, captured my imagination as a little girl, whereas I see you as an incredible man who I'm giving my love to as a woman unconditionally."

Conrad reached out, touching her cheek. "Then will you do me the honor of becoming my wife? Before you answer, let me say that I personally don't give a damn where we live, so long as it's together."

Audrey's eyes watered. "Yes, I will do you that honor, sweetheart," she promised. "I'll be equally honored to have you as my husband. And I know Stacy will be just as thrilled to have you as her father."

He hit her with a brilliant smile. "Well, then, shall we have a Christmas Day kiss to seal the deal?"

"Consider it sealed, Mr. Pearson."

Audrey leaned over and planted her lips on Conrad's, taking pleasure in knowing this would become habitual.

USA TODAY bestselling author

BRENDA JACKSON

TONIGHT AND FOREVER

A Madaris Family novel.

Just what the doctor ordered…

After a bitter divorce, Lorren Jacobs has vowed to never give
her heart again. But then she meets Justin Madaris, a handsome
doctor who carries his own heartache. The spark between
them is undeniable, but sharing a life means letting go of the
past. Can they fight through the painful memories of yesterday
to fulfill the passionate promise of tomorrow?

"Brenda Jackson has written another sensational novel…
sensual and sexy—all the things a romance reader
could want in a love story."
—*Romantic Times BOOKreviews* on *Whispered Promises*

Available the first week of December
wherever books are sold.

ARABESQUE®

www.kimanipress.com   KPBJ0231207

He was like a new man...

TO LOVE A STRANGER

Award-winning author

ADRIANNE BYRD

When aspiring fashion designer Madeline Stone's husband
returns after being lost at sea, Madeline is amazed that
Russell is no longer the womanizing rascal she married.
He's considerate, romantic...and very sexy.
Now Madeline faces a dilemma....

"Byrd proves once again that she's a wonderful storyteller."
—*Romantic Times BOOKreviews* on *The Beautiful Ones*

*Available the first week of December
wherever books are sold.*

KIMANI™
ROMANCE

Sometimes parents do know best!

Essence bestselling author

LINDA HUDSON-SMITH

*F*ORSAKING ALL OTHERS

They remembered each other as gawky teenagers and
had resisted their parents' meddlesome matchmaking.
But years later, when Jessica and Weston share a family ski
weekend, they discover a sizzling attraction between them.
Only, how long can romance last once they've left their
winter wonderland behind?

"A truly inspiring novel!"
—*Romantic Times BOOKreviews* on *Secrets and Silence*

*Coming the first week of December
wherever books are sold.*

KIMANI™
ROMANCE

www.kimanipress.com   KPLHS0451207

Bestselling author

Tamara Sneed

The follow-up to her acclaimed novel *At First Sight*...

At First
TOUCH

Daytime TV diva Quinn Sibley needs a comeback.
But first she needs to return to the man she left behind.
Wyatt Granger's still searching for Ms. Right—someone
quiet, shy and totally unlike this Hollywood siren who
haunts his dreams.

"At First Sight is a multilayered story that successfully
deals with sibling rivalry, family dynamics and
small-town psychology."
—*Romantic Times BOOKreviews* (4 stars)

*Coming the first week of December
wherever books are sold.*

KIMANI™
ROMANCE

following
LOVE

Award-winning author
Celeste O. Norfleet

Desperate for a job, single mom Dena Graham only has
one option—work for sexy, charismatic Julian Hamilton.
Julian has had enough of relationships and is focused
strictly on business…until Dena walks into his life.
Now these two, who've sworn never to gamble with
their hearts again, find that when red-hot attraction
enters the picture, all bets are off!

"A story that warrants reading over and over again!"
—*Romantic Times BOOKreviews* on *One Sure Thing*

Available the first week of December
wherever books are sold.

ARABESQUE®

A volume of heartwarming devotionals
that will nourish your soul...

NORMA DeSHIELDS BROWN

Joy
COMES THIS MORNING

Norma DeShields Brown's life suddenly changed
when her only son was tragically taken from her
by a senseless act. Consumed by grief, she began
an intimate journey that became
Joy Comes This Morning.

Filled with thoughtful devotions, Scripture readings
and words of encouragement, this powerful book
will guide you on a spiritual journey that will sustain
you throughout the years.

*Available the first week of November
wherever books are sold.*